ALL I WANT

J.H. CROIX

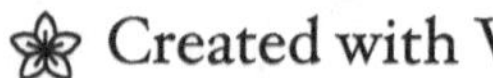 Created with Vellum

To friends, family & waiting for the right person!

Sign up for my newsletter for information on new releases & get a FREE copy of one of my books!

http://jhcroixauthor.com/subscribe/

Follow me!
jhcroix@jhcroix.com
https://amazon.com/author/jhcroix
https://www.bookbub.com/authors/j-h-croix
https://www.facebook.com/jhcroix
https://www.instagram.com/jhcroix/

ALL I WANT

Dallas

One kiss that burned so hot, I never forgot.
Five years later.
Audrey... the hottest woman I've ever known
and my sister's best friend.
I was half in love with her for years.
I moved on, and so did she.
The universe rolled the dice.
A dark, snowy night—no joke.
I find her walking through the darkness.
Christmas is right around the corner.
She's so d*mn tempting, I can hardly think.
Maybe rules are meant to be broken.
Maybe second chances are real.

Audrey

I've only fantasized about Dallas for, oh, too
d*mn long.
One wild kiss. Five years ago.
I've never forgotten it.
He's tall, dark and dangerous...for real.
FBI Agent, sexy man extraordinaire.
He couldn't be bothered with me.
Maybe because he thought I was too young.
I'm not anymore.

Chapter One

DALLAS

Snowflakes floated down from the night sky, skidding off my windshield as I drove north. I rolled my neck from side to side in a weak attempt to ease the tension bundled there. The digital clock on my dash told me it was past midnight, and I'd not so wisely left Boston when it was already dark for my drive to Maine. Through the darkness, the highway sign loomed. Haven's Bay showed clearly in the darkness, the light snow doing little to obscure the view. The moment I saw the sign, tension unspooled inside me. Haven's Bay was the place I went when I needed to get away, although I hadn't been here in almost four years. It was home in a way that nowhere else was.

A short trip on a side highway and then I was traveling through the quiet downtown. Holiday lights glimmered through the falling snow. The town might as well have been straight out of a postcard with old colonial homes lining its streets, trees decorated with lights and a tall Christmas tree standing in the center of town. No one was around. Hell, who would be at this hour when it was barely above ten degrees outside and snowing?

A winding road led out of town, and I turned off onto another long road. This was past the lovely, manicured part of town where the locals who'd been here for years and years lived. It was a mix of mansions and beach cottages. Lobstermen and fishermen rubbed elbows with the wealthy in Haven's Bay. The common link was their love of the ocean, their family's roots here in Maine, and the hardiness to stand strong through the harsh winters.

I passed by a car half in the ditch. I slowed to check to see if anyone needed help, but whoever had slid off the road was gone. I figured someone else had come along to help.

Despite the cold, I rolled my window down, savoring the salty scent of the ocean rushing through the window. I turned down a familiar driveway. I was about halfway down when my headlights illuminated a figure walking down the drive. My focus had been hazy because I was absorbing the feeling of coming home. Otherwise, I'd have noticed the lone pair of footprints along the side of the drive sooner. Everything sharpened. Aside from desperately needing a break from work, I was here in Haven's Bay for a reason. An old family friend had asked me to check on their home over the holidays. There'd been a rash of burglaries in the area in recent months.

I slowed to a stop beside the person, rolling down the passenger side window.

"Excuse me, you're..."

I meant to tell the person they were trespassing. My words petered out when I saw who it was. My heart lunged, and my mouth fell open.

"Audrey, what the hell are you doing here?"

I swung into action, climbing out quickly and walking around to her. So many questions tumbled through my mind, I didn't know where to start. I took the heavy bag she had clutched in her hands.

"Dallas?"

"Yup. It's me. I'm sure I have more questions than you, but let's get you inside."

She was covered in snow and visibly shivering despite her fluffy down jacket. Worry rolled through me. It made no sense for her to be walking through the snow in the dark, much less for her to be here. I surmised the car in the ditch belonged to her. She didn't resist when I opened the passenger door and all but shoved her inside. Once I was back in the driver's seat, I cranked the heat up, flicked the interior light on, and looked over at her.

She pushed her hood back with a sigh and turned toward me. Her dark brown hair was damp on the ends, and her hazel eyes looked weary in the soft light. My entire body tightened. I hadn't seen her in five years, and she was as beautiful as ever. With her wide eyes, her high cheekbones, her slightly crooked nose that tipped up at the end, and her lush, full mouth, she was an odd combination of regal and endearing. Oh, and sexy as hell.

I knew where she was supposed to be and where everyone believed her to be, and it most certainly wasn't here in Haven's Bay. It was her father who had asked me to come check on their family home. Her family had long since moved away from here year-round, yet they'd kept the home. I'd grown up just down the street. Our families had been friends until my family blew to bits, but that was another story. Right now, I knew Audrey was supposed to be in Italy on a skiing vacation with her fiancé. In fact, her father, Warren Edwards, had mentioned just last night they'd miss her for the holidays.

"Hi Dallas," Audrey said, her words falling softly through the hum of the heaters blowing over us.

She peeled off her gloves and held her hands in front of the heat, her gaze dropping from mine.

"Aren't you supposed to be in Italy?"

She looked back at me. Bitterness and pain flashed in the depths of her eyes. She swallowed, the sound audible in the small space of the car.

"I'm not."

"Clearly."

I waited. I was very good at waiting. I also didn't mind silence, no matter how tense it was. This helped immensely in my job as an FBI agent. Most of the time, I loved my job. I savored the chance to sit down with criminals in the interview room and outwait them through the heavy silence until we talked in circles to the heart of whatever dark matter they were tangled within. My skill in interviews and in leading investigations had gotten me promoted quickly through the ranks. This past year had worn on me as I'd overseen an ugly web of an investigation related to human trafficking. My specialty was in untangling financial fraud and money laundering cases. Sometimes following the money led to very sad places.

Right now, the small mystery of why Audrey wasn't in Italy swept the cobwebs of those worries out of my mind. I welcomed something else to fill the space.

"I found out he was seeing someone else," she said, her tone level and flat, as if she was consciously wiping it clean of emotion.

Anger scored through me—hard and fast.

"Matthew was seeing someone else?" I asked, my calm, controlled tone belying the fury I felt inside.

I'd fucking hunt him down and make him pay. Later though. Not now. Not with Audrey sitting beside me, pain coming off of her in waves. I sensed it because I knew her. Too well for my own good.

She was almost always level and controlled. Once, only once, had I seen her let go of her precious control. No matter how hard I'd tried to shove that memory away, it was rather insistent. Audrey was forbidden to me, or so I'd convinced myself. I also wanted her more than any woman. *Ever*. I'd pushed her away because I'd felt I must. Her family meant too much to me. Five years ago when she was home for the summer from college, I'd let things go too far. We'd come so close to fucking, it had taken more discipline than I'd known I had to put a stop to it. She'd been glorious when she let go. I vividly remembered the feel of her slick channel pulsing around my fingers. I gave myself a hard mental shake.

She nodded, her gaze fixed out the window. There was nothing to see but the snow falling softly, and the wind occasionally sending it in little swirls in the darkness.

"He's a fucking idiot."

She looked back at me, weariness lining her features, and lifted one shoulder in a graceful shrug. "It doesn't really matter. Can we get to the house?"

There were so many things I wanted to say, but she was clearly exhausted. That much was obvious. I nodded quickly and started driving. When I said the driveway was long, I meant it. It was almost a full mile long. I used those moments until we reached the half-circle at the end to rein in my fury at Matthew. I needed to pummel the guy, and even then I'd still be angry. Yet, that anger wouldn't do much for Audrey, and Matthew was nowhere near here.

That was another thing I was good at—compartmentalizing. Tucking emotions and details away to save for when the time was right.

I rolled to a stop in front of the house. It might've been five years since I'd seen it, but it was just as I'd remembered. A charming cottage with trees clustered to one side and a lawn stretching behind it. I would be able to see the ocean waves crashing against the rocky shoreline in the morning.

"Wait here," I said before hopping out and jogging through the snow on the front walkway.

I kicked my boots on the threshold as I stepped inside. I quickly turned on some lights and the heat. Spinning to head back outside, I found Audrey dragging her bag out of the back of my SUV. I snagged it from her.

"So much for waiting," I said, hoping to annoy her.

She straightened and rolled her eyes. Perfect. I'd rather her be annoyed than see that bitter, sad look in her eyes just now.

I grabbed my bag out of the back, hooking them both in one hand. She walked alongside me, kicking at the snow on the slate walkway with her boots.

In short order, we were inside. She went upstairs to shower, while I took stock of what was available in the kitchen.

I spun around when I heard footsteps. Audrey stood there, her glossy brown hair falling around her shoulders. She wore a faded sweatshirt and cotton pants that clung to her curves.

My cock twitched, and I ignored it. Just because I wanted Audrey and had ever since she'd been old enough for me to think about her that way didn't mean I could have her.

She crossed her arms and eyed me.

"Tell me why you don't want me," she said, her eyes flashing and dark.

Her question was so out of the blue I was unprepared. A bolt of lust hit me so hard, it nearly buckled my knees. Thank fuck I was standing beside the counter.

Chapter Two

AUDREY

Dallas Tate stood before me—in all of his ridiculous, sexy glory—and opened and closed his mouth, his hand curling around the edge of the counter.

Good. I'd rattled him. That was no easy feat.

Dallas had starred in far too many of my fantasies. Once, only once, had he given me the slightest clue he might want me as much as I wanted him. The clue involved the best orgasm I'd ever had, thanks to his expert fingers. But no sex. Right when I'd reached for the buttons on his jeans, he'd shoved me away so fast, I literally fell off the bed.

Without a word, he'd left the room. I hadn't spoken to him for a full year after that.

I'd been visiting my parents one summer between semesters in college and scrounged up the nerve to finally do something about the pent up desire I felt for him. Dallas had been the older boy-next-door all through my childhood. He was almost a decade older than me and so tempting, I'd have done just about anything to have him. But he'd made it crystal clear he didn't want me. Thanks to his family moving away, I'd rarely seen him. In fact, except for one brief encounter the following summer, I don't think I'd seen him until now. Five long years since my best orgasm.

I'd told myself I had to move on. So I had. Or rather, I'd convinced myself I had. I'd finished college and then law school. I'd dated here and there and gotten engaged, thinking I should. Matthew had been so charming. Clear-eyed, I knew I'd never experienced the white-hot passion with him that I'd felt with Dallas, but I'd talked myself into thinking that was a fluke, that I'd overblown my recollection of how I'd felt about Dallas. Seeing Dallas now for the first time in years was a brutal reminder of how foolish I was.

I was all a muddle inside. I was furious at Matthew and so mortified. Just my luck to get engaged to a cheating asshole. Even worse, I'd broken up with Matthew a month ago. He'd begged me to reconsider and persuaded me not to formally call off the wedding. Then, I'd walked in on him fucking one of my friends. Maybe it made no sense, but Matthew doing what he did had brought my thoughts full circle to Dallas.

Why, oh why, did I have this terrible habit of falling for guys who didn't want me? Dallas held the highest stature in that regard. He was the pinnacle of *unavailable and not interested* as far as I was concerned. I'd conveniently forgotten just how much I wanted him. For example, tonight. He pulled up beside me in the snow. I was cranky, upset and exhausted. One look at him, and I wanted to climb in his lap and ride him. It didn't matter how tired I was.

Instead, he treated me like family. Like he always had. I knew it didn't make sense to stomp down here and demand answers, but I wanted them. Maybe if I knew why Dallas couldn't be bothered with me, then I could figure out what it was about me that came up short.

"Well?" I asked, staring at Dallas and hoping he couldn't tell I was flushed.

Oh. My. God. He was too hot. With his black hair damp from the snow, his piercing blue eyes locked to mine, and his face looking like a damn sculptor's dream with his square jaw, his blade of a nose and his lips with that dimple in the middle, it just wasn't fair. His sleeves were rolled up, one forearm boldly decorated with a stark, black tattoo. He carried a day's shadow, the dark stubble only adding a dash of roguishness to the whole picture.

He was quiet for a few beats before his shoulders rose and fell with a deep breath.

"Mind telling me where this is coming from?"

"Me. It's coming from me," I snapped. "Don't try your annoying interview diversionary tactics on me. I'm not some criminal you're investigating. I have one question, and it's quite simple."

"That wasn't a question. It was more like an order," he countered, his lips curling at one corner.

My belly flipped, and heat rolled through me. I'd forgotten how potent Dallas was. Time and distance had faded the memory of what it was like to be near him. His presence was so powerful, my body lit up inside whenever he was near.

I realized I was drifting inside. I narrowed my eyes. "Fine. It was an order. Explain," I said, circling my hand in the air.

"Audrey, I haven't seen you in..."

"Four years," I added helpfully.

"Can we just have some dinner and..."

Emotions were roiling inside of me, little earthquakes of all kinds of feelings rocking me. Anger mingling with insecurity colliding with pain and tangling with desire. Matthew's betrayal was enough to deal with. Yet, in a strange way, my feelings about that were straightforward—I was angry, but I'd get over it. Dallas stirred up a storm inside of me— too many years of longing, fierce desire, the sting of his rejection, and the wish I didn't want him the way I did.

"No. We can't just... whatever. I'm tired and I'm upset. I just found out my fiancé is fucking someone else, and I want to know why. What's wrong with me? I'm not enough for him, and I obviously wasn't enough for you. I want to know why!"

Dallas stared at me across the kitchen, his gaze so intense, I got nervous. I was going a little crazy inside. I'd thought I'd be alone here. I'd been planning to lick my wounds and figure out how to tell everyone my engagement was off once and for all. Instead, my stupid car broke down. Then, Dallas just had to show up and save the night. Or something like that. Well, he didn't really save me. I only had about a mile left of my walk through the snowy night.

My anger suddenly dissipated, leaving in a whoosh. I took a deep breath and let it out. "I'm being crazy. Just forget I said anything," I said, turning and waving my hand. "I'm gonna crash. I'm exhausted."

I took about two steps when I felt his hand close around my arm. He spun me around so quickly, I stumbled and fell against him. Bumping into his chest was like bouncing against granite. The only difference was he was warm and strong and alive. It felt so good to be close to him. My breath caught when I collided with his gaze. His eyes were a rich, deep shade of blue, like the ocean on a clear day. They flashed with something, and I suddenly felt his cock, every hard inch of its length pressing into the cradle of my hips.

Oh. My... Panty-melting God.

"It's impossible to answer your question," he said, his words coming out sharp and clipped.

"It wasn't a question. It was an order," I said, surprised my words came out so clearly.

His mouth, that sinful, sexy mouth, curled into a wry grin.

"Okay, I can't follow your order then."

"Why not?"

My question came out breathy while my heart beat so hard and fast, it hurt.

"Because I can't lie to you."

"I don't know what you mean."

His eyes searched mine, looking for what I didn't know. I was an open book. At least I had been to him once upon a time. I'd told him how much I wanted him. I'd thrown caution to the wind, boldly walked into the house where he was staying that summer, and done my damnedest to seduce him.

My efforts had gotten me an absolutely glorious orgasm, but that's it. He'd left me there and told me to get the hell out before he returned.

"You know exactly what I mean," he returned tightly after a few taut moments.

"No. Actually I don't. What would you be lying about? You told me to get the hell out and leave you alone the last time this came up."

He stared back at me before nodding sharply.

"So I did."

"So what would you be lying about?"

All the while through this little back and forth, time felt suspended. The air around us was heavy, weighted with the desire I'd shoved deep into the recesses of my body, heart and mind. While desire wasn't a mind thing—hell if it were, I wouldn't be here wanting him more desperately than my next breath—it was tangled up in my thoughts because I'd had to use those to bury what my body so desperately wanted. Meanwhile, I felt the press of his cock, hot and hard, at the apex of my thighs.

Dallas shook his head slowly. "You have no fucking idea how much I want you."

His words came out in a growl and then his lips crashed to mine.

Chapter Three

DALLAS

I wasn't thinking. At all. Raw need roared through me. All I knew was I wanted Audrey. Now.

Inside of a minute, our kiss went from a flash point of contact to hot and heavy. With her tongue tangling with mine, it was all I could do to force myself to put a stop to it. Thank fuck my phone rang. Tearing my mouth from hers, we stared at each other. With her face flushed, her lips swollen and her eyes wide, it took enormous restraint to keep from kissing her again. I supposed she expected me to say something. I didn't know what the hell to say. I spun away and snatched my phone off the counter, only to see her father's number flash on the screen.

"It's your dad. I need to take this. He asked me to come check on the house. I'm assuming you don't want me to let him know you're here," I said quickly before answering.

She nodded tightly. I got through that phone call on the habit of manners. I let Warren know all was well with the house. He chatted about a few things and wondered whether I might reconsider and drive down to see them in the Berkshires for Christmas. He couldn't know I was riddled with guilt through the entire few minutes we were on the phone. If he hadn't called, I couldn't have stopped that kiss for anything. My cock was still throbbing.

As soon as I ended the call, I turned to see Audrey waiting. Her cheeks were flushed, and her lips swollen. Fuck. I should not have kissed her. I'd all but set my body on fire with need for her, and I needed to get a handle on it.

"Why did you kiss me?" she asked suddenly, her words clipped.

I leaned my hips against the dining room table, shoving my hands in my pockets. There was no sense in lying. "Because I want you."

Her mouth dropped open, and it was all I could do not to snatch her against me again.

But I needed to stay sane. Before I had a chance to formulate what I meant to say—whatever the hell that was—Audrey spoke.

"How can you say that? Last time..."

"Last time, I put a stop to it because you were barely twenty! You're my sister's best friend."

The words flew out, and I knew I sounded angry. I was. Not with her though. With myself. I took a ragged breath and ran a hand through my hair. "Audrey, your father means a lot to me. I can't..."

This time she cut me off.

"Oh my God! Okay, forget about how old I was then. I'm twenty-five years old now. I'm not some foolish young girl. I wasn't then either. And what the hell does my father have to do with anything?"

I stared at her, my thoughts spinning.

Five years ago, I kissed Audrey in the stupidest, craziest moment I'd let myself give into. We'd both grown up here in Haven's Bay, our families close for years. Audrey was nine years younger than me, so all the way through college and until I moved away to Boston afterwards, I'd thought of her as nothing more than the young daughter of my parents' friends. She grew up and nearly knocked me over the first time I saw her when she was nineteen. With her glossy dark hair, her flashing hazel eyes and curves for days, I almost hadn't recognized her.

At a glance, you might think I'd been the lucky one. My family was wealthy, very wealthy, and had been for generations. My great-grandfather had made his money through shipping and timber. His fortune came from honest work and the luck of timing. Like many families generations ago, he came to the United States with not much more than what he'd scrabbled together for the ride across the Atlantic. He'd worked on the docks in Boston, worked on the ships and gradually worked up to buying his own and expanding it into a fleet. He'd invested his earnings from shipping in the timber industry here in Maine.

Haven's Bay was roughly midway up the coast in Maine. My family had a lovely home with a gorgeous view of the ocean within a mile of this cute, but much smaller home where Audrey had grown up. This home had been a caretaker's cabin on my family's property many, many years back. My grandparents had sold it to her grandparents. Her mother was a teacher, and her father a lawyer. Audrey was now a lawyer as well. Her family was nothing but respectable, smart and hard-working. The long friendship her parents had shared with mine had been blown to bits a few years ago. Thanks to me.

I grew up in that gorgeous home on the windswept coast of Haven's Bay. Inside the walls of that home, my father was fucking asshole. He'd been distant with me and my three younger siblings my entire childhood. Love was hard to come by, if at all. Affection and approval were doled out in money only. I figured I'd never know what happened between my grandfather and my father, but my dad was nothing like him. Instead of believing in hard work, he believed he was entitled to wealth without any effort.

My specialty area within the FBI related to financial crimes. I'd been heading up a regional case, chasing down lead after lead in a sprawling money-laundering case. Unfortunately, one of those leads brought me straight to my father. His preference for living off of investments eventually pushed him into creating a Ponzi scheme after a few investments went awry. I'd had to completely step back and hand the case over.

He now sat in jail. What little relationship we had was severed, and he lost most of his friends, including Audrey's parents. What money my family had left had been confiscated. Unbeknownst to me, my father had signed our family's home over to me before everything blew up. I was still torn with what to do with the home. I loved it dearly, but I was furious with my father. My mother had died years back from a stroke, so it fell to me to handle the logistical mess for my three younger siblings.

That was the ugly story for my family. Audrey's father was more of a father to me than mine had ever been. Hence, my guilt over the fact I wanted Audrey like I'd never wanted any woman. *Ever*. My guilt wasn't that she felt like family. Because she didn't. We had been nine years apart growing up. When things went to hell with my father, her father had been a huge source of support. I felt sick to contemplate what he would think if he knew I was harboring the secret of Audrey's presence here. He'd be heartsick to learn her engagement had blown up.

I had stifled my desire for Audrey and put it away behind lock and key. I'd been a bit relieved and simultaneously disappointed when I learned she was engaged sometime last year. If I couldn't have her, I wanted her to be happy. The wedding was supposed to occur next summer. The second my mind spun in that direction, a flash of anger coursed through me. Fucking Matthew. I'd never met the guy. Now to learn that Matthew had been seeing somebody on the side, I wanted to make him pay. Seeing as he was nowhere near, that was a problem for another time. The problem at hand: the fact I wanted her so much I could hardly stand it, and she was here.

Now she was waiting for me to explain. "Audrey, you know how much your father means to me. I can't..."

She rolled her eyes. "I'm an adult. I can be involved with whoever I want." She paused and shook her head. "Look, I'm tired. I don't have it in me to make sense of anything right now. I came up here to get away, but you're here."

I let my breath out slowly. I'd take the break on trying to discuss that crazy kiss. But I didn't want her to think she had to take off just because I was here. "I doubt you figured your dad would ask me to spend the month here. Obviously, we can both stay here."

As soon as I said that, I wondered if I was flat crazy. Yet, I couldn't exactly tell her to leave. If I called her father and told him I was leaving, he'd wonder why. In short, the easiest thing to avoid curious questions was to carry on as we'd respectively planned. I just hoped like hell she didn't plan to stay long.

She stared at me, her eyes weary, and I had to hold back from tugging her into my arms again. It wasn't simply lust when it came to Audrey. Never had been. Yet, now wasn't the time. I'd already mucked things up enough.

After a long moment, she nodded. "Fine. I'm crashing."

She spun away without another word.

———

I walked down the stairs the following morning, relieved to find Audrey wasn't up yet. Making a beeline for the coffee pot in the corner of the kitchen, I quickly started a pot of coffee. I wasn't used to waking up in a house with anyone, much less Audrey. I'd kept my hunger for her locked in a tight corner in my mind and in my heart. After four years of conveniently not seeing her, I'd somehow convinced myself I'd moved past my response to her. I didn't know what the fuck I was thinking last night when I kissed her. It had been a colossal mistake.

But damn it felt so good. Merely thinking about it now, I had to grip the countertop and will my thoughts off of the way Audrey's lips felt under mine to keep from getting hard all over again. Just like I knew from the memory I had saved and rarely allowed myself to think about, she was wild and unrestrained when she kissed. So much of me wanted to take things as far as they could go with her, solely for selfish reasons. I wanted her. All to myself. Yet, aside from the complications of my guilt because of her father, I wasn't a good candidate for any kind of serious relationship. My life was my career. It left little room for what I knew I wanted with Audrey. I forced my mind off of her.

I needed to shift gears and come up with a plan, specifically a plan that involved her not being here for the entire month I was supposed to be here. Whether that meant me leaving or finding some way to get her to leave, it needed to be one or the other. There was no way I could tolerate a full month here with her. The temptation would be too great.

The coffee maker beeped, and I spun around. I filled a mug with straight black coffee, exactly how I liked it. I took a few sips before jogging out to my car. In the surprise of finding Audrey last night, I hadn't unloaded the car. I carted in some file boxes for cases I was working on, along with my laptop. I set up a workstation at the dining room table and sat down to plow through my email. I might be taking a month off from active duty on cases, but I would be monitoring and doing online work from a distance.

I was scrolling through my email when I heard footsteps on the stairs. I took a gulp of my coffee, bracing myself. Audrey walked through the archway and looked over at me. Seeing her was like a kick straight to my chest. My pulse rocketed and my entire body tightened. This response was the very reason I'd found it convenient to avoid holiday visits with her family ever since that fateful afternoon when she'd caught me off guard and I'd fallen prey to the desire beating like a drum in my body.

Her glossy dark hair was damp and fell straight over her shoulders, brushing the tops of her breasts. I might not be able to see them through her loose T-shirt, but I knew exactly how they felt against me. I had a vivid memory of the weight of her breasts in my palms. Because that's how far I'd let things go that one afternoon five long years ago now. She'd been only nineteen years old at the time, while I'd been looking ahead to thirty. If anything, she'd only gotten more alluring in the time since. Her hazel eyes caught mine as she stepped across the room and slipped into the chair at an angle across from me.

She flipped her hair off her shoulder and met my eyes. Damn. I could've lost myself in her eyes for days—layers of green, gold and nutmeg, the color shifting the way shadows moved in the trees and leaves fluttered in the wind.

"Good morning," she said simply, her voice husky with sleep.

Thank fuck I was seated at the table, which hid my instant erection. I took another sip of coffee. "Morning. There's coffee in the kitchen if you'd like some."

"I might get some in a minute. What did my dad say last night?" she asked.

After his call and our brief talk, she'd gone to bed, which had been for the best. I'd needed her out of sight to get a grip and to keep my hands to myself.

"He was checking to see how my drive went and if all was okay with the house. If I didn't explain last night, your dad asked me to stay for the month until after the New Year passes," I explained.

Audrey nodded, idly twirling a lock of hair around her finger. "Yeah, he's been worried about those break-ins in the area."

"Reason to worry from what I hear."

Haven's Bay, like many coastal towns in Maine, had plenty of houses that sat empty all winter. They were prime pickings for thieves looking for a quick buck and things to sell.

She glanced around the room, her eyes coming back to me. "Well, the house seems fine."

"I did a check around last night except for your bedroom. Everything is as it should be. I'm assuming you would've said something if there was something amiss in there."

She nodded quickly. "Of course. It's fine."

She went quiet, still twirling her hair around her finger, her eyes watching me.

"I didn't know you would be here. I hope you didn't mention me to my dad," she said, her eyes worried.

"I told you I wouldn't. I figure that's up to you."

I forced myself not to offer more. I generally took a blunt approach to difficult or painful topics, probably a side effect of being an FBI agent. I spent so much time addressing topics that sent many people to jail I found it easiest to cut to the quick. But this was up to Audrey. Not me. Not to mention I had my own personal reaction to it. She didn't need my fury at how Matthew had wronged her to affect how she wanted to handle it.

She bit the corner of her bottom lip, worrying it in her teeth. Not helpful at all for the state of my cock at this point. I took another gulp of coffee and willed myself to think of anything other than Audrey sitting here in front of me, available and quite clear about the fact she wanted me, if last night was anything to go on.

"Do you plan to let your family know what happened soon?" I finally asked.

One shoulder rose and fell in a graceful shrug, her gaze watchful and guarded. I hated that look in her eyes, hated knowing she was worried what anybody thought about what had happened. Matthew was the asshole. She had nothing to be embarrassed about. Good riddance as far as I was concerned. She was better off with someone else.

Exactly. How about you? She wants you and you sure as hell want her.

Shut the hell up. I can't have her.

You're the only one saying you can't have her. In fact, her father would probably love for you and her to be together. At least he could trust you.

My job takes up too much of my life. There's not much room for anyone, certainly not Audrey who deserves far more than I could ever give her.

Only you can love her the way she deserves to be loved.

Fuck. I gritted my teeth and willed my mind to stop debating these points. That summer after she tried to seduce me and halfway succeeded, I'd had hours and hours of mental debates over her—what she meant to me, and what I could and couldn't do about it. In the end, what finally stopped the debates—to be honest, they never stopped but they quieted down—was when everything blew up on my case and the breadcrumbs led straight to my father. The upheaval of my family being shattered and torn apart by my father's actions had taken up all of my emotional energy.

"I don't know when I'll tell them," she finally said, her husky voice piercing my thoughts. "I will. I just wanted a few weeks to myself before I did."

"How long are you planning to stay here?" I asked.

"I was supposed to be in Italy for a month. Now I'm here, and Matthew's there and my phone won't stop ringing," she said, pain and anger flashing in her eyes.

I looked at her phone, innocuously sitting on the table where she'd set it when she sat down.

"Is he calling you?"

It took an act of will to keep my voice calm. I was furious with Matthew to see the pain in her eyes.

She nodded. "Yeah. I guess he didn't expect screwing one of my bridesmaids to interfere with our plans."

Chapter Four

AUDREY

I looked over at Dallas. His deep blue eyes were locked to mine. I sensed the anger coiled tight inside of him. No matter what I wanted, no matter our kiss last night and all the confusion I felt inside, I savored his anger and the way it made me feel protected. I was furious, but I was also mortified and embarrassed that any of it had happened with Matthew.

"Are you telling me he was cheating on you with one of your friends?" Dallas asked, his voice low and taut.

I took a breath and let it out with a sigh. Snagging my phone off the table and opening the screen, I spun it around for Dallas to see the row of calls from Matthew.

I wasn't sure what Matthew had expected when I found out he'd been screwing Alyssa, but it was clear he hadn't expected me to dump him. Social impressions were important to Matthew, something that had annoyed me the entire time we'd been involved. He wouldn't appreciate explaining our abruptly cancelled engagement and wedding.

Matthew had been a compromise in my mind and in my heart. Dating in general had been a compromise. There was only one man I'd ever truly wanted and that man sat across from me now. His eyes narrowed as he looked down at the screen on my phone. He looked back up at me, and my breath caught.

"Block his number," Dallas said flatly.

A flash of anger rose inside. I was a mess emotionally. I'd driven all the way to Haven's Bay yesterday. From New York City, it was a solid eight-hour drive. Add a little snow and my car breaking down, and I'd had way too much time to be alone with my thoughts. Having Dallas show up had only made my emotions more raw.

"Why do you care?" I asked.

He lifted his chin and arched a brow. "No matter what you think, I care about you. Even if I didn't and you were a random stranger, I would tell you to block his number. He's a fucking asshole. How long was he seeing someone else?" he asked sharply.

Restless, I stood. "I need coffee for this conversation."

I walked quickly into the kitchen, aimed straight for the cabinet and poured a cup of coffee. I liked my coffee dark, just like Dallas. I hated that I knew little details like that about him. But I did. I wished I'd forgotten. I'd sure as hell tried over the last five years after he made it abundantly clear he wasn't interested.

I spun to the kitchen window, looking outside for a moment. The lawn stretching towards the ocean was covered in snow. Waves rolled up against the rocks to one side of the beach, misting the air. I took a deep breath. I loved this place. It was home to me and always would be. I'd told myself I could make a life away from here with Matthew in New York City. We met when I was at law school at NYU. I'd tried my hand at dating here and there through college and law school, but none of it had been great. Matthew was the first guy who really tried to woo me. He'd pulled out all the stops. Even now, I had to admit he'd done quite the job— flowers, candlelit dinners, flattering me with compliments and then some.

I let out a small, bitter laugh thinking about Dallas' question about how long Matthew had been fucking Alyssa. I didn't have an answer to that. I was supposed to fly to Italy the day before him because he allegedly had a big case to wrap up. My flight was canceled due to the weather, but not until the last minute. I'd returned to our apartment to find Alyssa tangled up in the sheets with him. In our bed.

My bitterness was compounded by the fact I'd tried to call off my engagement with Matthew a month prior. We hadn't had sex in months, and the distance between us had grown to a chasm. Matthew had sweet-talked me into giving it another try the weekend before and bought us tickets to Italy. It should've been a clue that we still hadn't had sex in that week, but we'd both been working grueling schedules, or so I'd thought.

I'd torn my ring off, thrown it on the floor and left. I'd asked no questions, and I didn't really give a damn about his explanations. Too much betrayal on too many levels. I took a gulp of coffee, savoring the bitterness.

———

Returning to the dining room, I slipped into

the chair at an angle from Dallas. One glance in his direction, and I had to will my pulse to slow and my traitorous body not to have such a powerful response to him. Why oh why did I have to want him so much?

I took another gulp of coffee and set it down. He was reading something on his laptop. He glanced up, closed it and looked back over at me. With his deep blue eyes searching my face, I shifted in my chair, restless and hyperaware of my body's reaction to him—heat spiraling outward and need tightening in my belly. I tried to take a deep breath, but it wasn't particularly effective. Air was hard to come by when my pulse was going wild with Dallas's attention fully on me.

I hoped perhaps he had forgotten his last question of me, but I knew better. He angled his head to the side.

"How long?" he asked.

"I don't know actually."

I quickly summarized the events of my afternoon and evening yesterday. His eyes darkened when I explained I had walked in on Alyssa and Matthew. He didn't say a word, but I could feel the fury coming off of him in waves. He felt controlled and coiled tight. A hot shiver raced through me. It shouldn't turn me on to have him be protective and angry on my part, but it did. I should be more heartbroken over Matthew. Yet, I wasn't. I was just plain angry and embarrassed. I wasn't heartbroken because what I'd been trying to call *love* for Matthew was only a lukewarm version of what I felt for Dallas.

Dallas had held that place in my heart and in my body for too long. No one else elicited the same feelings inside. I'd probably managed to convince myself I'd moved on because I hadn't seen him and had forgotten how powerfully I was drawn to him. As soon as I'd been old enough to be aware of men and notice them in a sexual way, he had dominated my fantasies. Five years ago, nothing more than a few minutes with him were etched into my body and mind as the hottest moments of my life. Those few moments had allowed me to think perhaps he returned my feelings, or at least my desire.

My mind flashed to last night—the feel of his lips against mine, and his cock, hot and hard, cradled at the apex of my thighs. My heart, my silly, silly heart, spent most of last night as I barely slept obsessing over what it meant that he'd been turned on. I gave myself a mental shake. Not the time or place to go there. Not with Dallas, the subject of way too many fantasies, sitting right across the table from me, his far too perceptive gaze on me.

"So what are you planning to do?" he asked.

"I broke up with him. I left, and I don't intend to change my mind."

There were many doubts crowding my mind, but not that. I was done, completely done, with Matthew.

"Why do you think he's calling you?"

I laughed and took a sip of coffee, my laugh more bitter than the dark flavor.

"I don't know. Matthew likes things to look good," I explained. "I'm guessing he's worried that it won't look good that I'm not in Italy with him for the month and that I've called off our wedding."

Dallas nodded slowly, pausing to take a sip of coffee. "Good, I'm glad you're not having second thoughts. Are you listening to his messages?"

"No, I think I'll take your advice and block his number."

I picked up my phone and did just that. Matthew wasn't worth it. Not when he'd been a compromise to begin with. When I looked back up at Dallas, he nodded firmly in approval. For a flash, I was annoyed again. I hated that he was right and that I should just cut Matthew out of my life with surgical precision. If I were being honest with myself, I hated how much Dallas meant to me and how much I wanted from him when I knew he returned none of my feelings. Except for desire perhaps.

"I would imagine you would call your family at some point in the next day or so if you were in Italy. Am I right?" he asked, his tone careful as if he wasn't sure how I might react.

"I suppose it's best if I don't string them along and let them think I'm in Italy," I replied with a sigh.

His eyes were carefully blank. "I'd say not. I'm assuming Matthew could be in touch with them, and it's probably better if they hear from you what happened rather than his version of events. Not that your parents would believe him over you, but it's always better to establish the narrative."

I idly traced the edge of the placemat in front of me, taking another sip of coffee. I wasn't worried about my parents believing whatever bullshit story Matthew might concoct, but I didn't want them to be concerned. My chest and stomach had been tight with anxiety and anger since yesterday when I walked in on Matthew and Alyssa. The sensation hadn't faded after seeing Dallas. His presence had only thrown something else into the mix. The ache in my heart and anxiety in my belly were for wholly different reasons.

I stood and walked to the dining room windows. We had a bay window that looked out into the trees. Snow was still falling softly. It had snowed throughout the night with several more inches piled on the lawn.

"How much food is in the kitchen?" I asked, spinning around to look at Dallas.

"Not much," he said with a shrug. "I was planning to head into town for a run to the store in a little bit. Is there anything you'd like me to get? I'm also guessing that car I drove by last night on the side of the road was yours."

I sighed. "Yup, it is. I suppose I need to deal with that today."

"My SUV can probably get it out of the ditch no problem. We can take care of that before I go into town."

I laughed a little. Of course Dallas was prepared. He always was.

"What's so funny?" he asked.

I shrugged, feeling my cheeks heat a little. "I should've known you'd be prepared. I bet you have a tow cable and everything."

His gaze never wavered. "Of course."

"Well, maybe we can deal with my car and then go to the grocery store together."

The moment I spoke, I wondered what the hell I was thinking. I needed to come up with a plan. I couldn't allow myself to stay trapped here with Dallas. I had intended to stay here for a few weeks and then head down to see my parents in the Berkshires. Those plans had not included Dallas being here. With my ego wounded and my doubts about my desirability in general crowding the front of my thoughts, the last thing I needed was too much time alone with Dallas.

No matter what though, I wasn't leaving today. I was too tired from the drive yesterday and the snow was still coming down. Looking out over the ocean, I could see the gray clouds extending as far as the eye could see.

Dallas was standing before I finished my train of thought. "Let's do it. We'll take care of your car first and then we can run to the store. Anything else you might need in town?"

I shoved my worries about coming up with a plan to the back of mind and went upstairs to get my snow boots.

Chapter Five

DALLAS

Several hours later, I stood in the grocery store in Haven's Bay, listening to Audrey as she chatted with Sherry Levesque. Sherry and her husband Emile had owned Haven's Bay Grocery, along with a few other businesses in Haven's Bay for as long as I could recall. Come winter, the population in Haven's Bay thinned considerably. Those who stayed year-round were always happy to see other locals make an appearance in town. Though Audrey, like myself, didn't live here anymore, she'd been born and raised here so she would forever be considered a local. Sherry was peppering her with questions about her job, New York City, and how her fiancé was.

Audrey somehow managed to keep the conversation going without directly lying about the fact she'd just broken off her engagement. I felt for her. I knew she didn't want to get into that with Sherry. If anyone in Haven's Bay found out she'd called off her wedding, her parents would be getting a phone call before sunset.

Sherry belatedly looked over at me where I stood with the grocery cart. The cart was filled to the brim. While Audrey and I hadn't discussed it, I'd shopped for what I needed for the month. I'd yet to come to a decision about how to handle her presence here, but I wasn't backing out on my commitment to her father to stay here for the month and keep an eye on things. As we'd shopped, she'd tossed a few items in the cart.

Being with her like this was harder than I'd imagined. Hard could apply to more than one thing at this moment—difficulty, or the state of my cock anytime she was too close to me.

"Well Dallas Tate, it's so good to see you," Sherry said warmly. "How are Noah, Ian and Thea?" she asked, referring to my two brothers and my sister.

"Good to see you too, Sherry," I said,

resting my elbows on the cart. "Noah's busy in DC, Ian's working so hard I barely talk to him, and Thea's still busy in New York City doing the legal thing."

Sherry nodded along as Audrey and I started unloading the groceries for her to ring us up. As we chatted with Sherry, one question that never came up was how my father was doing. Everyone in Haven's Bay knew he was in jail. He'd fleeced many of them in his financial scheming, so the betrayal ran deep. The only reason old family friends didn't hate me too was because I'd sold off many of our family's assets to repay people.

It didn't slip my notice that Sherry's gaze bounced between Audrey and me a few times. She was clearly curious. It certainly wasn't unusual for Audrey to be in town. It wouldn't be suspicious that we would still be friendly. Yet, the last time we'd both been in Haven's Bay at the same time had been over four years ago. We'd certainly never spent much time together outside of the circle of our families. Once she'd grown up and become so damn tempting I could hardly stand it, I'd done my best to only encounter her when other people were around.

As I drove back toward her family's

home, the snow was picking up its pace. It felt as if a nor'easter was on the way, which meant the wind and snow would pick up significantly in the next few hours. Despite my apprehension at having Audrey here, I was relieved she hadn't chosen to leave yet. If she were to return to New York, she had quite a drive. From the forecast we heard on the radio, all of New England would be hit with the storm tonight.

The Christmas lights stayed on during the day in Haven's Bay, glittering through the gray snowy afternoon as we drove through downtown and headed out onto the coastal road. I kept my eyes on the road, only occasionally glancing sideways at the ocean view. There wasn't much to see today with the snow falling and waves rolling into the shore. The horizon was nothing but shades of foreboding gray.

Once we'd put away the groceries, I was at loose ends and uncertain what to do. I needed to keep myself busy with Audrey around, so I settled down at the dining room table to work. She went into the kitchen, reporting that she planned to cook something.

The wind picked up its pace, along with the snow. By early evening, it was a white-out storm. I stood up to stretch and walked to the windows to look outside. Nothing but swirling snow could be seen.

I heard Audrey answer her phone. As soon as she said hello, her tone ratcheted up. Concerned it was Matthew even though she'd blocked his number, I went to stand in the archway leading into the kitchen.

"Alyssa, I can't believe you're calling me. What the hell do you want?"

Audrey's hair was tied up in a messy bun, loose tendrils falling down around the nape of her neck and her face. She wore a long sleeved, fitted cotton shirt that buttoned in a V over her swingy cotton pants. She was clearly dressed for comfort, yet every curve was easily visible. At least to my eyes. What I couldn't see, my imagination filled out because I knew how she felt against me. Her cheeks were flushed as she gestured while she talked.

"There's no explanation that makes any sense. Alyssa, you were fucking my fiancé!"

She hadn't seen me yet and rolled her eyes in response to whatever Alyssa said.

"No! I don't want to talk about it. He's all yours as far as I'm concerned. That's what you want, right?"

I held back the urge to grab the phone from her and tell off the faceless Alyssa. I didn't even know her. I figured she was a friend of Audrey's from law school or college. I was painfully familiar with her social orbit here in Haven's Bay. For one, she was close friends with my younger sister. Once she'd become so alluring I could hardly take it, I hadn't been able to help myself from noticing every detail about her. All the way down to the crowd she ran with in the summer, the guys whose eyes followed her when she walked down the beach, tanned and way too curvy for her own good.

"Alyssa, forget it. You made your choice when you did what you did. Why would I want to work something out with the guy that fucked one of my friends who was going to be in our wedding?"

Every word Audrey said came out sharp. She huffed, muttered something and then tossed the phone. It slid across the end of the counter and fell to the floor with a thump. I stepped into the kitchen and picked it up.

"I suppose we should've blocked Alyssa's number too."

Audrey's eyes whipped up to mine, anger and pain flashing in their depths. I hated the pain. She spun away, wrapping her arms around her waist.

"I suppose so," she muttered. "I'll do it now."

She spun back around and strode quickly to me, snatching the phone from my hands, her movements jerky. When she got close enough, I saw the glimmer of tears in her eyes, and my heart clenched. I held myself back from tugging her into my arms.

She quickly opened her phone. There was a fine tremor in her fingers, and it made me angry all over again. Damn Matthew and Alyssa straight to hell. I watched as she tapped her screen and quickly blocked Alyssa's number.

"Was she a good friend?" I asked, my tone husky.

Fuck. It killed me to see her like this. Audrey took a shaky breath, carefully setting her phone back on the kitchen counter before looking up at me.

"Well, she was supposed to be one of my bridesmaids. She's not my best friend if that's what you mean. Thea was going to be my maid of honor," she explained, referring to my little sister.

"Does Thea know what happened?" I asked.

Audrey shook her head sharply. "No. I didn't call anybody yesterday."

As I stared down into her eyes, seeing the pain flashing in the depths and the fine tremor running through her, the tight grip I had on my control slipped for a beat. I pulled her into my arms. All I meant to do was comfort her. I swear. She stiffened for a moment and then relaxed against me. She didn't sob because that wasn't her way. I heard her taking shaky breaths against my chest, all the while my heart thundered with a visceral ache. I didn't know how much Matthew meant to her, but he hurt her and I hated him for it.

Sadly, the effect she had on my body was too powerful even for this moment. Feeling the lush curves of her breasts pressing against my chest and the warmth of her, my cock throbbed. I knew she could feel it, and I couldn't bring myself to step back just yet. I focused on holding her and hoping somehow she would absorb what I was trying to convey. It didn't matter what had happened. It wasn't about her, it was about a man who didn't know an amazing woman when he had one.

Somewhere along the way, Audrey's arms slipped around my waist. She lifted her head, her eyes locked into mine, darkening as she looked at me. What I'd meant to be a comforting hug was turning into something else entirely. The space around us felt electrified, fairly vibrating under the force of desire between us. Fuck me. I wanted her so damn much. She took a shaky breath, her eyes locked into mine.

"Just so you understand, it's not like I was in love with him. I think I talked myself into it. I also tried to break things off, but he persuaded me to hold off," she said softly.

I arched a brow. "Well, then why were you going to marry him?"

"He was really nice at first. I figured he was the best I would get."

"What the hell do you mean, Audrey? The best you could get?"

She never looked away. "I'm not the kind of woman most men go for. I don't back down in a fight, I don't spend time stroking anyone's ego, making them feel smart and strong. That's not my personality and you know it. Plus, like I told you once before, there was always somebody else that I wanted more," she said, that bitter look entering her eyes.

It was the same look I'd seen last night when she demanded I tell her why I didn't want her. I was normally a rational, calm man. I thought everything through. I considered contingencies and looked ahead to the potential consequences of certain actions. I didn't get to where I'd gotten as an FBI agent by being impulsive and acting on emotion. Rather, it was the opposite. I was never impulsive, and I never let emotions drive my actions.

Right here, right now with Audrey held against me, I suddenly made an impulsive, probably stupid decision. No matter what happened, she would know that I wanted her. She'd never forget it. I stared at her, the air around us becoming so heavy my cock hardened to the point of pain.

"Don't ever compromise. Not for a man," I said flatly, my voice coming out almost in a growl.

I lifted a hand and brushed a loose lock of hair away from her cheek, tucking it behind her ear. Her breath hitched, and I could feel her nipples, tight little points, pressed against my chest. My body answered, and I pulled her even closer, sliding my palm down her spine to cup her bottom and bring her against me. My cock was buried at the apex of her thighs. I could feel the heat of her there. Her lips parted, and her eyes widened slightly, darkening as she stared at me. The raw desire in her gaze answered mine with such force, I couldn't deny it. I dipped my head, again damning myself straight to hell. I might not be able to have her as completely as I wanted, but I would have this. If only so she would know for once and for all...she was completely wrong about me not wanting her.

Chapter Six

AUDREY

The moment Dallas fit his mouth over mine, it was an electric shock to my system, straight to my core. His tongue swept deeply into my mouth, tangling with mine. I was burning up inside. He devoured my mouth with his. His hand tangled roughly in my hair, his other palm cupped my bottom and pulled me against the hard, hot length of his cock. I curled a foot around his calf as I roamed my hands over his back and chest. I needed to feel him. All of him. Now.

I gasped when his hand slid around to cup my breast, thumbing my nipple. My nipples were tight and achy. I was hot and prickly all over and close to frantic. I hadn't felt like this in five years, not since the last time we kissed. Unless I counted last night, but that was so fast and so shocking, I'd hardly absorbed it.

His lips blazed a trail down my neck. Between kisses and soft nips, he muttered my name and hot dirty words. I barely caught anything he said, only the intensity. For now, I didn't care about anything other than my need to nearly meld myself with him. He lifted me against him easily. When he took a few steps, I lifted my head. There was barely any space between us. His hand gripped my hair so tightly, I couldn't look away. His touch was rough, and it struck the chord of wildness in me that needed him like air.

"Where are you going?" I murmured.

The grip of his hand in my hair tightened, and I savored the sharp tingle of pain in my scalp. I needed the bite of desire to slice through me, to help me forget all of my doubts. My legs were curled around his hips, and his cock rode hard and hot against my clit. I couldn't help but roll into him.

"Fuck, Audrey," he muttered darkly. "Slow down."

He leaned back, his dark blue gaze colliding with mine. He loosened his hand in my hair slightly. His eyes were electric, the space between us weighted with pent-up need and longing. He slid his hand out of my hair to cup my nape, his thumb tracing along my jawline and around my lips. I caught it in my teeth, biting down softly. I was restless and needy, ensnared within the sharp intensity of this desire.

"I don't want to slow down," I murmured, my voice barely above a whisper, roughened by desire.

His eyes searched mine. I might have doubts about many things, but right here, right now, I didn't doubt what I felt between us. Whether it was just raw desire or more, I didn't care to contemplate. I needed to whet my appetite. If it would only be once with him and that's all I would ever have, I would take it.

"Where are you going?" I repeated, only then releasing his thumb from between my teeth as I stared at him.

I swiped my tongue across my lips. They were swollen, bordering on sore, from the ferocity of our kiss.

"Bedroom," he said simply.

We stared at each other for a few beats.

"It appears I have a point to prove," he said, his voice a gruff whisper.

"Point to prove?"

He cupped my bottom and arched into

my hips. There was no mistaking the hard, hot length of him pressing into me. The layers of clothing between us were nothing.

"You seem to think I don't want you."

"Because you sent me away before, and you've ignored me ever since," I said flatly.

I was beyond caring about much of anything now. I'd already embarrassed myself so thoroughly with him once, it couldn't get any worse this time.

"I didn't want to send you away, but we can't have each other, not that way. We can have this."

"Sex?"

He nodded sharply, his eyes dark.

"Is that all you want?"

Despite how controlled his expression was, I knew him. I knew him the way you do when you grow up with someone. He wasn't family, but he was damn close. I saw something flicker in the depths of his eyes.

"That's all this can be," he said flatly.

My heart clenched. I knew he wasn't involved with anyone. Thea, his sister and my closest friend, had often complained he hardly even dated. I knew from her that his work was his life. She worried about him. Thea had never known of my long-ago crush on him, a crush that had gone unrequited.

She also never knew about my attempt to seduce him.

That silly mistake had cemented the depth of my desire for him. He was also an honorable man. I knew quite well what his family had gone through over the last few years once everything blew up with his father. I knew the pain it had caused his entire family. I knew from Thea he had done everything he could to make things right, to atone for his father's sins. That only made me want him even more. All of these thoughts tumbled through my mind as I stared at him, realizing that he was offering me only the chance to be close to him in this way. He was carefully trying to draw a line for me. I didn't know how I felt about that, but I knew I wanted him.

With my heart drumming in my body and heat rolling through me, I held his gaze and nodded.

"Take me upstairs."

He moved swiftly, his hold on me never wavering. I savored the flex of his muscles against me as he carried me. I busied myself tasting the warm skin of his neck. I loved the smell of him—sharp and clean with a hint of pine. As he shouldered through the door of the guest room, I briefly wondered why he chose this room and not mine. My thoughts were lost in the turmoil of sensation. He eased me down and set to stripping off my clothes.

He was nothing if not efficient. Before I knew it, I was down to nothing but my panties. His gaze swept over me, lighting fires everywhere his eyes landed on my body. I hadn't been quite as efficient as him, but I had managed to get his shirt off. My mouth went dry at the sight of him. I'd seen him bare chested before, but not this close. He was cut and fit, always had been. A jagged scar ran along his upper shoulder on the right side. I briefly wondered where it came from, a flash of worry running through my mind. His job wasn't exactly safe, but those questions would wait for later. I followed the line of the dark, bold tattoo curling in strokes down along his upper arm and around his elbow. Another tattoo feathered along the edge of his ribs on his side. I wanted to trace the lines with my tongue.

I reached for him, hooking my finger in his belt loop and pulling him toward me. I lost my balance, my hips falling to the bed. His mouth curled at one corner, that devilish grin sending my belly spinning. I was wet, so wet I had to clench my thighs together to quell the ache there. I distantly considered that sex with Matthew had never even come close to the way I felt with Dallas. Any orgasms I'd had were the result of my own efforts, not his. I was so close now, I knew all Dallas would have to do was sink inside of me, and I would probably explode around him.

He put his palm on my chest, his touch hot. The calloused surface of his fingers brushing across one of my nipples sent a jolt of want through me so hard and fast, I lost my breath.

"Come here," I said, restlessly shifting my legs.

His eyes darkened, but he was quiet. With gentle pressure, he pushed me back on the bed and stretched out atop me. My legs curled around him, and I savored the rough feel of the denim against the insides of my thighs. He kissed me again, long slow and deep. I forgot my impatience and tumbled into the moment. Deep strokes of his tongue, his teeth catching my bottom lip when he drew away, his eyes locking to mine, his gaze alone setting me afire. His hands charted my body. Every press of his hips against my sex arced the need higher and higher inside. It felt like the underside of a wave, the water rushing out to sea, pulling it fast and hard underneath, coiling it into a ball of power tightening in my core.

His lips made their way down my body, dallying at my breasts, rolling one of my taut nipples between his thumb and forefinger while he laved the other one with his tongue. I was murmuring incoherently between gasps. Out of my mind with need, I could feel the wet silk between my thighs.

"Dallas, please..." I murmured.

He lifted his gaze, his teeth closing over my nipple. I cried out at the bite of pain, savoring it.

"I'm getting there," he murmured, the gruff sound of his voice alone sending a shiver through me.

He shifted his weight, hooking a hand over the edge of my panties and yanking them down my legs. He tossed them to the floor and then settled down, his mouth coasting across my belly—hot, wet kisses, the occasional scrape of his teeth. His hand stroked up my thigh, a finger sliding through my folds.

"Fuck, you're so wet Audrey," he murmured against my belly.

I felt drugged, so out of my mind with need. I could barely speak, so I didn't even try. My head fell back on a low moan when he sank his finger inside of me, my pussy clenching around him. The wave inside was coiling tighter and tighter. I could feel it reaching its crest. He dropped kisses on the insides of my thighs, making me cry out, the skin so sensitive every touch was almost too much. With a dip of his head, he dragged his tongue over my clit. A spike of pleasure shot through me. Gripping his hair in my hands, I was rough, but it was all too much. Another finger joined the first, and he set his mouth against me, exploring my folds with his tongue.

I hadn't thought I could take anymore, but somehow I did. Dallas kept me right at the edge, right where everything was coiled tight, ready to let loose and break. I murmured his name and begged—yes, I begged. Finally, another swipe of his tongue across my clit and the pleasure crashed through me, spinning and tossing me in its current.

I dimly heard him standing, the rustle of clothes falling to the floor and the tear of foil nudging me out of my haze. I looked up at him.

"Dallas, come here."

Chapter Seven

DALLAS

Audrey lay before me, the covers a mess and the pillows tossed asunder around her. Her skin was damp and flushed with passion. With her dark glossy hair spilling out across the pillows and her eyes locked to mine, my knees almost gave out. I'd forgotten every single reason why I told myself I could never have her. All I knew was this moment with her. Finally kissing her again for the first time in years was like coming home. She struck a chord I hadn't even known existed. It ran deep and true inside of me. No one else could satisfy it. I let myself soak in the sight of her. I'd only imagined how she looked bare naked for years. To see her now knocked the breath from me.

The length of her fit legs flared into lush hips. The dip at her waist only served to show off her generous breasts. Her nipples were taut and damp. One knee had fallen to the side, revealing her pussy, so pink and wet. I could still taste her on my mouth. Feeling her come against my lips had been close to divine. The insides of her thighs were wet from her juices. I swallowed, latching onto a thread of control.

"Dallas..."

Her husky voice set my heart to thudding against my ribs. I was coiled so tight with need, it wouldn't have surprised me if I came the moment I sank inside of her. I rolled the condom on in record time and stretched out over her again. Lacing my hands into hers and stretching them over her head, I glanced down. Her gaze was hazy and dark, an edge of wildness to it. She'd nearly torn my hair out when I'd had my face buried between her thighs. I didn't give a damn, she could go as wild as she wanted. As long as it meant I could be with her like this. I could feel the wet heat of her against my cock. I shifted my hips slightly, letting my shaft slide through her folds. She let out a low moan.

God, I fucking loved the sounds she made. This was now only the second time in my life I'd seen Audrey let go. For a flicker, I wondered if she was like this with other men, with Matthew. Jealousy hit me so hard and fast, I was almost stunned. Jealousy was not a feeling I was familiar with. Work was my life. Women only occupied a sliver of my time. I shoved the thoughts away and shifted again.

I arched into her again, savoring her wetness sliding against me. "Now would be the time to let me know if we're taking this too far," I murmured, leaning up slightly.

She curled her fingers into mine, gripping tightly and shaking her head back and forth.

"Don't you dare stop now," she ordered.

I laughed softly. "Wasn't planning on it."

I adjusted the angle of my hips and sank inside of her, groaning at the feel of her creamy clench around me. She was so hot, so wet, and so tight, it felt incredible. Far more incredible than I could've imagined. I'd now crossed the barrier I'd refused to allow myself to cross before. I knew once I had, I'd never be able to walk away. I didn't think about that now, I simply allowed myself to get lost in the sensation of her. I held still for a moment, allowing her body to adjust to me. At the feel of her hips arching into me, I started to move, easing back and then sinking deeply. Long, slow steady strokes, burying myself to the hilt again and again and again. She curled her legs around my hips, rising to meet me with every thrust, crying my name out, demanding I go faster, gasping that it wasn't deep enough, begging me for more.

I meant to drag it out, determined for this to be everything and more so she'd never forget it. She was having none of that. She tore her hands loose from mine, her nails scraping down my back. Murmuring incoherently, she arched into me, her teeth sinking into the bottom of my neck. Lust lashed at me, and I lost control, my hips drumming into her. Her channel started to throb and pulse around me. I felt when she tumbled over the edge, crying out my name. Damn, it was the sweetest sound I'd ever heard.

My own release hit me so fast and hard, I lost my breath. It whipsawed through me, and I collapsed, spending myself inside of her. We lay tangled up in each other, skin to skin, sweaty, hot and out of breath. I could've stayed there forever. After a few moments, I felt her skin start to pebble. I started to draw back, and she tightened her legs around me.

"Don't," she murmured.

My heart clenched. "Not going anywhere, but it's cold. Let's get under the covers."

I looked down at her, her skin flushed and

sweaty, her eyes still dark and her lips swollen. My stubble had roughened the skin on her neck.

I trailed the backs of my fingers over the reddened skin. "Did that hurt?"

Her mouth curled at one corner. "I don't know. I didn't notice," she said softly.

She slowly loosened her legs, and I eased away, standing and stepping into the bathroom off the guestroom. I tossed the condom in the trash and quickly returned to the bed. Tucking us under the covers, I fell asleep with her twined against me. Breathing in the scent of her, I wondered if I'd just made the biggest mistake of my life.

Because there was one thing I knew with certainty: I'd never get enough of her.

Chapter Eight

AUDREY

Hands on my hips, I glanced around the kitchen. I had completely forgotten I'd been in the middle of prepping to make chicken dumpling soup last night. That's how thoroughly Dallas had wiped my mind clean. Obviously, I never returned to the kitchen and finished. I sent up a silent thanks I hadn't taken the chicken out yet because that would've been a smelly waste. As it was, I had left chopped carrots and celery out on the counter overnight and nothing more.

I smiled a little, my cheeks getting hot. I couldn't quite believe last night had happened. My pulse kicked up a notch just thinking about the feel of Dallas buried inside of me. I'd woken this morning, warm in his arms. He'd been curled up behind me, his palm resting on my belly. The air outside the covers had been cool as it always was during the winter here. I'd felt his arousal pressing against my bottom. Perhaps I should've felt uncertain about what might happen next, seeing as he'd made it quite clear sex was all we could have. Yet, he hadn't said just once.

So, I spun in his arms and rolled over, sitting astride him. When his eyes had opened, sleepy and hooded, that rich blue gaze locked on me. We tumbled back into another heated interlude. We'd showered together, and he was presently in the dining room working. His work phone had buzzed insistently on the nightstand this morning.

I told myself that perhaps he had put a limit on what we could have, but he hadn't put a limit on how long that could last. I intended to wring every last drop out of this that I could.

It was snowing and blowing outside, so I shifted gears, cleaning up what I started last night with plans to make the chicken dumpling soup for dinner tonight. For breakfast, I prepped omelets. Once the coffee was ready, I poured a cup and carried it out to Dallas.

He glanced up from whatever he was

working on, flashing me a quick smile and taking the cup from me. His fingers brushed against mine, and electricity zinged through me. I spun away, my belly fluttering, and returned to the kitchen. I had one omelet in the pan when there was a loud knock at the front door. I heard the scrape of Dallas' chair before he strolled into the archway leading to the kitchen.

"Expecting anyone here?" he asked.

"Aside from you and Sherry, nobody knows I'm here."

He arched a brow and shrugged. "I'll go see who it is."

As he stepped away, it occurred to me he was quite right I needed to call my parents and let them know where I was. I didn't need them to get confused and worried if they found out from someone else I wasn't in Italy and I'd called off my wedding. I heard the sound of the door opening, Dallas' low voice and then Matthew's voice.

Oh no. This could not be happening. I didn't hear the door close, so I waited. I wondered what Matthew was going to try to say to Dallas. They had never met, although Matthew would likely connect the dots if only because he knew Thea and knew Dallas was her brother. I heard the murmur of Dallas' voice and Matthew sounding slightly belligerent, but not raising his voice too much.

Cold air blew in from the front entrance. After a moment, I heard the door close and then one set of footsteps in the hallway. Dallas leaned into the archway between the dining room and kitchen, his eyes on me.

"That was Matthew," he said, his voice clipped.

I could sense his anger and couldn't help the flare of satisfaction it gave me. I was angry with Matthew for the most obvious of reasons, yet a part of me savored the protective quality of Dallas's anger on my behalf.

"Does he know I'm here?"

Dallas shook his head sharply. "No. I'm glad we put your car in the garage. If he'd seen it, I think he'd have tried to make it ugly. I hope it's okay I told him to stay the hell away from you."

I stared at him, my mind spinning, my gut churning, and my heart clenching. It infuriated me to have Matthew come up here. I didn't know why he was chasing me. Yet, it was Dallas who made my heart clench. I didn't quite know how to react to his protectiveness.

I took a breath, staring at him across the room, and nodded.

"Of course it's okay. I don't want to talk to him. There's nothing to say."

Dallas was quiet, his eyes considering.

"My advice?" he asked, only a hint of question in his words.

I laughed a little. I'd heard him offer unsolicited advice to Thea many times over the years, and he always led with that question.

"Sure, Dallas. What's your advice?"

"I know I just told him to stay the hell away from you, but you might want to go ahead and talk to him. My guess is he's going to keep after you unless you do. He strikes me as pushy and entitled. He doesn't get it."

Dallas couldn't have known just how accurate he was in his assessment. But then again, he probably knew quite well. His job relied on him reading people very, very well.

"Now? Is he waiting on the porch?" I asked, my eyes widening.

My gut was tying itself in knots, anxiety blooming in my chest. I wasn't up for this. Not now. This morning had been too good, and I didn't want Matthew to ruin it. He had no right to think I would talk to him. About anything. He'd lost that right when he fucked one of my friends *after* sweet-talking me into giving him another chance.

Dallas shook his head, laughing a little at my expression.

"Nah, I sent him off and told him you weren't here. He whined that he didn't know where to stay, so I suggested a few places the next town over. He said he flew into Bangor. Seemed to think he'd find you here and said he had a ticket for you to return with him."

I rolled my eyes and turned away to flip the omelet. Of course, Matthew would be that arrogant. My mind flashed to the sight of him in our bed with Alyssa on top of him. We hadn't had sex in months. Our lack of intimacy was what led to me attempting to break things off with him. I was still annoyed I'd given in to his persuasion to give things another try before I called off the wedding. Although, I supposed I might never have discovered the truth about him cheating if I'd held firm. I'd chalked up our lack of sex and growing distance to both of us being busy with work. He'd been working long days and late into the night on a big case.

Just now, I realized his 'big case' might've been Alyssa the entire time. Nothing but regret twisted in my heart over that. I wished I'd had enough sense not to accept the personal compromise I'd made over Matthew. I'd known what we had was nothing like what I felt with Dallas, yet I'd figured it was the best I'd get. I shoved those thoughts away. Nothing to do about it now. I couldn't change the past, no matter the folly of my choices.

I turned the burner off and slid the omelet onto a plate, spinning back to face Dallas. He was waiting patiently, his eyes on me. The moment was heavy and quiet, feelings crowding the room. I considered what to do. I couldn't quite believe I was in this situation. My ex-fiancé who'd been screwing one of my bridesmaids had chased after me. Meanwhile, the man I'd never quite forgotten stood before me. Years of unfulfilled longing had finally culminated in the most amazing night of my life. With him.

Dallas was here offering advice about what to do about my ex-fiancé. There were many things I wanted to ask, most of them nothing to do with Matthew. I knew Dallas was right though. Better to get my conversation with Matthew over with sooner rather than later.

"Where did he go if he's not standing outside?"

Dallas looked over his shoulder and spun around, walking through the dining room to the front windows facing the driveway.

"Still sitting in his car actually. I'm

guessing he doesn't know where to go. Do you want to talk to him now or later?"

I considered my options. I'd rather call Matthew and meet him somewhere in town than let him sully this space with his arrogance. It felt as if Dallas and I were in our own little cocoon here, and I wanted to keep it that way.

"I'll call him later and maybe meet him somewhere in town for lunch or dinner."

Dallas walked back toward me, glanced over his shoulder once more as he did.

"Looks like he's leaving." His blue gaze landed on me again. "How about I go with you?"

"You mean when I go talk to Matthew?" I asked, puzzled as to why he'd want to do that.

He nodded as if it were a perfectly reasonable thing to do.

"Dallas, that's going to be weird."

"Why?" he countered.

"Um, because he's my ex-fiancé and last night, well, we..."

My words ran out. I felt my face get hot and wished I didn't blush so easily.

His mouth curled at one corner, sending my belly into somersaults.

"We did a lot last night. And this morning," he said, his low voice sending a shiver over my skin. "What does that have to do with Matthew?"

"I was engaged to him until a few days ago."

He nodded slowly. "Yeah, and he was fucking one of your friends on the side. What does he have to do with us?" he asked.

I stared at him across the room, uncertain how to respond. "I guess nothing. It's just going to be weird to have you there. You guys don't even know each other."

"So? I don't want him to be an asshole to you," he said bluntly, his eyes narrowing.

My chest suddenly felt tight. I didn't quite know how to handle his protectiveness of me. It felt so good, but I didn't want to read too much into it. After a few beats, I shrugged. What the hell? It was going to be an awkward conversation no matter what type of spin I put on it. It was no less worse to have Dallas there than it was to try to do it alone. Dallas was quiet. His gaze was too perceptive, so I turned away, quickly pouring the eggs for the next omelet into the pan. I was restless and needed to keep myself busy and away from the disconcerting feeling of his eyes seeing right through to the core of me.

"I don't have to go," he said, his voice coming from over my shoulder.

I felt his presence as he stepped closer. My heartbeat stuttered and then leapt when his hand slid down the center of my back, resting at the dip of my waist. That simple touch was both a turn on and a comfort. If only I'd known how much I would crave his touch, I might've had more sense than I did last night. I didn't quite know how to be with him in this space this morning. It was easier when we were tangled up in each other. I could lose myself in sensation, in the intimacy that ran so deep it shocked me.

I sprinkled shredded cheese in the omelet, flipped it quickly and then lined vegetables in the center and more cheese before folding it. I loved to cook and right now it gave me something to do other than think about how close Dallas was to me.

"How about you let me know what you want me to do?" he said softly.

I finally glanced to my side. His eyes were right there waiting, the heat in them sending a jolt of need through me. My sex clenched. Sweet hell. All we were doing was standing there while I made an omelet. For God's sake, we were talking about my ex fiancé who'd been screwing one of my friends.

There were so many reasons I should be anything other than turned on. That was how powerful my response to him was. For a flash, it occurred to me this was crazy. I shouldn't have let anything happen last night. Because walking away from this would be hard, incredibly hard.

I was still staring at him when he arched a brow, nudging me to recall he'd asked a question.

"You can come," I finally said.

"You sure?"

I swallowed, willing my pulse to slow.

"Yeah. You pegged Matthew right. He's an entitled jerk. Honestly, I knew that and I just ignored it. He'll want to badger me, but if you're there, he probably won't."

I glanced down at the omelet and flipped it again before turning the burner off.

"Are you ready for breakfast?"

He stared at me before his mouth curled at one corner. "Of course."

My belly did a slow flip, and I wondered again if I was crazy.

Chapter Nine

DALLAS

I walked at Audrey's side into the restaurant, wondering if I was stone cold crazy to be here. Thinking back to this morning, I reminded myself yet again Audrey had a crazy effect on me. She held the unique ability to keep me from thinking clearly. I knew why I wanted to be here. I'd taken one look at Matthew and sized him up for the idiot he was. I could admit I was biased against him from the start. Before I knew he'd been fucking one of Audrey's friends behind her back, he'd represented the man who had the one woman I truly wanted.

No matter how hard I'd tried to keep from wanting her, I still wanted her fiercely. The compromise I'd come to in my mind was if she was in love with another man, and he took good care of her, I would be able to let go of the hold she had on me. The potency of the memory of her that long ago afternoon—hell, it couldn't have been more than ten minutes with her—would fade. Or that's what I'd told myself for the last five years. She would get married and work would be my life. Now I knew what Matthew had done, and I hated him for his sheer stupidity. The shallow arrogance it took for him to show up, chasing after her as if though she was suddenly important to him infuriated me. I wasn't particularly looking forward to this evening, but I didn't want to let him hurt her again.

That's not why you're here. You're marking your territory. You need to back the fuck off. You know you can't let things go too far with her.

I shook those voices away. Crazy or not, after last night, I wasn't about to let that be all I had with Audrey. I was usually a man with a plan, and I had none right now. None beyond allowing myself more of Audrey.

She stopped by the reception desk in the restaurant. Despite being in the dead of winter and still lightly snowing outside, Bay Bistro was busy. Haven's Bay might empty out in the winter, but Mainers prided themselves on being able to tolerate the hard winters. There were plenty of locals that stayed here year-round. Sherry Levesque caught my eye from across the restaurant. Sherry and her husband owned this place, in addition to the main grocery store and a few other businesses. You wouldn't know at a glance as they were quite down-to-earth and led a quiet life, but they were damn wealthy. Sherry's husband Emile had wisely bought up one business after another over the years. All of them were successful and made money hand over fist during the tourist season of summer.

I gave Sherry a wave and forced myself to let my hand fall off of Audrey's waist. I might be here with her tonight and fully intending to be with her later in more ways than one, but it wouldn't be helpful for Matthew to think we were anything other than old family friends. Years of being in the FBI had taught me quite clearly there were layers of lies and layers of truth. In this case, it was the truth that Audrey and I were old family friends. It was a lie of omission in allowing Matthew to think nothing more. He didn't need to know I'd been buried balls deep inside of his ex-fiancée last night. Part of me wanted to needle him with that knowledge. It would be easy to do. I wouldn't have to say a word.

Yet, I knew Audrey wouldn't appreciate

it. No matter what an asshole he'd been to her. She didn't need to deal with his petty grievances, and he was that kind of man. It wouldn't matter to him he'd been fucking one of her friends and Audrey had tried to break it off even before she knew that. If he had any suspicion she and I were together, he would turn it into something about that. Sherry greeted us with a smile.

"Well, fancy seeing you two again," Sherry said cheerily as she walked quickly to meet us.

Audrey nodded tightly, tucking her hair behind her ears, a habit she'd had since childhood. It was something she did when she was nervous. My heart gave a hard thump, and I had to force my attention to Sherry.

"We're actually here to meet Matthew," Audrey said.

Sherry's eyes narrowed. "Matthew?"

I breathed a silent sigh of relief that Audrey had called her parents' today. She'd kept her conversation short and assured them she was fine before handing the phone over to me when her father wanted to talk with me. He'd also kept it brief, simply asking if she was okay and asking me to let him know if she wasn't. With Audrey here to meet with Matthew, I knew word would spread once it became known she'd called off the wedding.

"I might as well just tell you," Audrey blurted out quickly. "I called off the wedding." Her words came out fast and clipped, two red spots appearing high on her cheeks.

Audrey wasn't one to worry too much about what people thought, but I knew she was a private person. Sherry's gaze softened.

"What the hell did he do to you, hon?"

Audrey shrugged. "It doesn't matter. It's for the best anyway. He showed up at the house today. I agreed to meet him here, just to make it clear it's over once and for all."

Sherry's eyes flicked to me. "Well, I'm glad Dallas is with you. Now that you've told me the wedding's off, I'll tell you what I think. He was never good enough for you. I'd hoped for the best for you, but I'm relieved to hear it's over," Sherry said bluntly.

Audrey's eyes widened slightly and then she took a breath and let it out with a sigh, her shoulders relaxing. I fought the urge to touch her again.

"Well, you were right," she said softly.

Sherry gave her a little smile and then stepped around the reception desk to give her a quick hug. "You'll be fine. You'll find the right man, and it will be everything you wanted." As she stepped away, she gestured to the back of the restaurant. "Anyway, he's already here. He acted like you two were still together by the way," she said with a roll of her eyes. She looked to me again. "Don't let him be an asshole to her."

I chuckled. "Absolutely not, Sherry."

Sherry took the extra step of walking us over to the table and introducing us to the waiter whom she gestured to follow as we walked across the restaurant. I knew she was doing it just to make a point to Matthew. Namely that Audrey meant a lot to her and that she had people here who cared about her.

My chest tightened a little at the controlled expression that fell over Audrey's face when she looked at Matthew. I wanted her to be angry. Hell, I wanted to haul off and punch the guy myself, but it would be more satisfying to have her let loose on him. Yet, what I wanted and what Audrey wanted might be quite different. It made me sad to think back to what she'd said yesterday about him—that she'd known all along she didn't quite love him and thought it was the best she was going to get. I felt a pang realizing I might be partially responsible for that state.

Sherry stepped away from the table, while

the waiter moved to fill the water glasses. Audrey slipped into the furthest chair from Matthew, which left me sitting across from him. She angled herself slightly closer towards my chair. I could tell by the look on his face he'd expected her to sit across from him. Fuck that. She chose to sit where she wanted.

"I didn't expect you to bring anyone," Matthew said. "I was hoping we could talk privately."

Audrey met his gaze, her chin lifting slightly and anger flashing in the depths of her eyes. "You forfeited that right," she said calmly, her tone perfectly polite.

Matthew cocked his head to the side. "Forfeited what right?"

"The right to a private conversation. If you wanted a private conversation with me, perhaps you shouldn't have been fucking Alyssa," she said, every word enunciated clearly.

I bit back a laugh. Okay, so this was how it was going to go. Worked for me. I leaned back into my chair. The waiter's eyes darted amongst us.

Audrey remained calm and measured. She looked up to the waiter and asked, "Can we go ahead and order some wine please?"

The waiter didn't miss a beat. He pulled

out a small tablet and flipped it open, quickly reeling off a few wine choices. Audrey selected a bottle and pointedly noted she would be sharing it with me and then looked to Matthew.

"Were you planning to order anything for yourself?"

Matthew's face was red, and his eyes dark. Amusement turned to anger inside of me as I looked over at him. He had absolutely no right to be angry with her about anything. The fact she'd even agreed to have dinner with him was more than he deserved. He ordered a beer and stayed quiet until the waiter departed from our table. He then looked to me.

"Do you mind? I really need to speak privately with my fiancée."

Audrey's hand curled around my arm, which was resting on the table.

"Dallas isn't going anywhere," she stated clearly. "I asked him to be here, and I'd like him to stay. Please stop referring to me as your fiancée. I am *not* your fiancée, nor will I ever be again. Our engagement is over, and the wedding is off. That is final. The *only* reason I agreed to meet you for dinner was to make that perfectly clear."

I beat back the urge to haul her into my lap and kiss her.

She proceeded to detail everything related to their wedding she had already canceled. I kept my approval silent, but I was proud of her. It might've been years since I'd seen her, but I hadn't forgotten her feisty side. She'd never been one to back down in a fight, and I was damn glad to see she still held that fire inside of her. I surmised she'd been busy while I was working earlier. She'd joined me at the table with her laptop for a bit, announcing she would be working as well. She must've been busy methodically canceling all of their wedding plans.

I carefully watched Matthew as she spoke, pausing only when the waiter delivered our drinks. I sipped my wine as she continued. Matthew looked furious, but he appeared to have enough sense to stay quiet.

"I'll send you a detailed receipt later from my lawyer," she said in conclusion.

"Your lawyer?" Matthew asked, a hint of snide in his tone.

"Yes, my lawyer. I know how you can be, Matthew. You like to win. I'm not even going to entertain any of your bullshit. We'll sort out who gets reimbursed for what, and who will be responsible for any costs that can't be refunded. Once that's done, you won't hear from me. Ever again."

I could see Matthew silently calculating, his eyes narrowed and his lips tightened in a line. He had no idea what he was in for. I'd known Audrey forever, and she had a temper. It didn't show very often, but when it did, she didn't back down. I was damn glad she wasn't backing down for him.

———

It wasn't long before Matthew decided to leave. He actually had the gall to try to hug Audrey, but she wasn't having it. Once he exited the restaurant, her shoulders relaxed. She took a gulp of her wine and looked to me.

"Well, that was a relief. I can't believe he thought there was any chance we might still get married."

I shrugged, my eyes on her. She'd worn her hair up in a twist this evening. It was pulled back tightly, not a single hair loose. Her hazel eyes were bright in the dim light of the restaurant. She wore a deep red sweater, the rich color setting off her fair skin and dark hair. I wanted to see her hair down. It was as if she'd pulled it back to bolster herself, to eliminate any softness to her. Before I realized what I was doing, I reached over and slid the clip out of her hair. It tumbled loose, the glossy locks falling around her shoulders. Her cheeks flushed, and her eyes widened. A startled laugh escaped.

"What are you doing?"

I took a swallow of wine before answering. I couldn't tell her I hadn't meant to actually act on my thought. I simply thought I wanted to see her hair down again. Apparently, I wanted it enough that my body acted on the impulse without consideration. Unsettled, I shifted my shoulders and looked back at her. "Your hair is beautiful," was all I said.

My mind spun back to earlier today. After Audrey had called her parents, she'd called Thea. I hadn't been privy to the details of that conversation because she'd gone upstairs to have it. She and my little sister had been best friends forever. Sometime after Audrey's call with Thea, Thea called me to check on Audrey. I was relieved at least to know Audrey wasn't hiding where she was. I had learned more than I probably should've known about the state of Audrey's relationship with Matthew before she found him with her friend. For example, I now knew that apparently they hadn't had sex in months. Thea had openly shared her relief that Audrey had called off the wedding. She even shared she'd suspected Matthew had been cheating on Audrey for months and had only stayed quiet about it because it was nothing more than a gut feeling.

As these thoughts tumbled through my mind, I considered my relief at knowing Audrey was free of Matthew. I hadn't reckoned with the truth of my jealousy of him before this point. Hell, I'd buried my feelings for her so deeply I'd successfully forgotten how much she meant to me. In particular, I'd forgotten how much I wanted her. *Want* didn't quite capture how I felt. It was more of a burning desire, so intense it nearly set me on fire.

Audrey took another sip of her wine and ran her fingers through her hair. Fuck me. Just that small action and my cock got hard. I wanted to lace my fingers in her hair and kiss her senseless. I told myself to keep my mind out of the gutter. She'd only just had her second conversation with her now ex fiancé since walking in on him fucking one of her friends. She might not be up for yet another night like last night.

She glanced over at me again, a smile

curling the corners of her mouth and her eyes darkening. "Thank you," she said softly.

I had to give myself a mental shake to remember what I'd just said. Oh yes, her hair. "Well, it is." I forced myself onto any topic other than how fucking beautiful she was. "How are you?" I asked, considering she might be relieved her conversation with Matthew was over, but there might be more to it.

She leaned back in her chair, angling her head to the side and shrugging. "Honestly, I'm fine. I mean, it sucked to walk in on him fucking one of my friends. But the whole situation's just shown me I never should've agreed to marry him in the first place. I don't know..." She paused, her cheeks pinkening again. She took a gulp of wine before continuing. "I think I tried to talk myself into it because I figured it was the best I'd find. Now that it's over, I'm realizing it was way too much of a compromise. I'd rather be alone than settle for someone like that."

My heart gave a hard kick, as if trying to get my attention. Audrey's unexpected appearance here and finally giving into my longing for her had knocked through the walls around my heart so thoroughly, I was scrambling to gain control again. Control of nothing more than the state of my own heart, body and soul.

I stared at her, keeping my expression calm. "Good. You shouldn't settle. For anyone."

Her eyes caught mine. She smiled and gave her head a little shake. "No, I never should have to begin with."

At that moment, our waiter came to clear our plates. "Anything for dessert?" he asked, his eyes bouncing between us.

Audrey glanced to me. I shrugged. If she wanted dessert, we would have dessert. At the moment, I was busy wrestling to get my body under control. I wanted her. Fiercely. Having her close like this with the subtle, sweet scent of her drifting to me, it was an act of will to keep my attention on socially acceptable matters. All I wanted was to pull her into my lap, kiss her senseless and bury myself inside of her. After a beat, she glanced back to the waiter.

"We're all set. I'll just finish this glass of wine. You can bring the check when you have a chance," she said.

He nodded, clearing the rest of our plates from the table and then spinning away to return to the kitchen. Sherry passed by, throwing a smile our way as she moved on to serve a bottle of wine for another table. I almost jumped when I felt Audrey's hand slide onto my thigh. I swung to look at her, watching as her eyes darkened.

"You know what I thought about today?" she asked.

Unable to speak, I simply shook my head, fighting to keep my cock from getting any harder than it already was. It was a futile effort. I was already rock hard, so hard I likely had an imprint of my zipper on my cock.

"When I was talking to Thea today, she told me she was relieved. I wished I'd ended things a lot sooner. She thinks Matthew has been seeing Alyssa for a while. I should've suspected it myself. But I've been busy with work and when Matthew told me he was working late on a big case almost every other night, I believed him. Now I know why we hadn't had sex for months."

I simply nodded, uncertain how to reply. When she didn't say anything and it was clear she expected me to say something, I asked, "Why are you telling me this?"

She shrugged, her hand still hot on my thigh and my cock still hard.

"I'm not sure. I suppose I wanted you to know that while we may have only officially broken up days ago, I wasn't really with him for months longer than that. I mean, my God, I tried to call our wedding off sooner, but he made me feel bad, like I wasn't understanding enough of how busy he was."

Next thing I knew her hand was on my cock under the table.

"Fuck," I muttered. "What are you doing, Audrey?"

She smiled slightly, her eyes sly. "What I want to do."

"We need to go," I said, my words coming out tight and low.

I cleared my throat and reached for her hand under the table. The last fucking thing I wanted to do was dissuade her stroking my cock through the denim of my jeans. But we were in a restaurant, and we needed to walk out. She rolled her eyes when I purposefully drew her hand away, keeping it held in the grip of mine.

"Spoilsport," she said with a little laugh.

Nothing more than the sound of her husky voice and seeing this bold side of her, and lust jolted through me. I signaled for the waiter with my free hand. Audrey quickly drained the remainder of her wine.

"I'm done," she declared with a sassy grin.

It would be a miracle if I got out of here without dragging her into my lap.

Our waiter delivered the check, and I paid in cash because I didn't want to wait. I barely gave her enough time to put her jacket on before walking out of the restaurant, her hand held tight in mine.

Chapter Ten

AUDREY

I savored the warmth and strength of Dallas' grip around my hand. So much had become crystal-clear in the last few days. Perhaps I was slightly crazy to let myself keep playing with fire the way I was with Dallas. This was nothing more than a fling, and I needed to remember that. Yet, I couldn't help myself. We were here together, and there was no one else to interfere with our time. I was going to wring every drop out of this that I could. Cold air hit my face when we stepped outside. The snow had finally stopped, and the air felt sharp and crisp. I paused for a second, looking up into the sky. Stars glittered in between wispy clouds drifting across the night sky.

I released his hand and spun in a circle. Bay Bistro was in the center of downtown Haven's Bay. It was lovely here at night in the winter. Holiday lights glittered, snow-covered tree branches reflected against the sky, backlit from the lights below. I took a bracing breath of air and let it out with a sigh. When I looked back at Dallas, his gaze was waiting, dark and unreadable.

I didn't know what he thought, nor did I know why I felt the need to explain to him that Matthew and I hadn't been intimate in months. I supposed that was more for myself than for Dallas. No matter how lukewarm things had been with Matthew, I didn't like thinking of myself as someone who would bounce from one man to the next in a matter of days. Somehow, it made me feel better to know that the writing had been on the wall with Matthew. If I were honest with myself sooner, I'd have seen we'd been nothing more than roommates really for months. Even at the beginning when he was charming, I'd never felt much more than a warm affection, nothing close to the explosive desire I felt when I was with Dallas.

As Dallas and I stood there staring at each other, he caught my hand in his again and reeled me closer to him. I came flush against him, gasping at the heat radiating from him. It was icy cold out, and he gave off heat that I wanted to burrow into. God, he felt so good—tall, strong, and solid, everything I'd wanted for so long. I hadn't quite realized how effectively I had stuffed my feelings for him into a corner. Perhaps because I hadn't seen him in so long. I had forgotten the potency of him, the raw power of his presence when we were close. His hand slid through my hair, sliding down to cup the nape of my neck.

"Should we talk?" he asked, his words low and taut, the sound vibrating through me.

"About what?" I whispered.

"This. Us. This thing we're doing."

I shook my head quickly. I didn't want to talk. I was afraid if we talked about it we would stop. We would each come to our senses and realize this was a dangerous game we were playing. Dallas had made it quite clear that all we could have was sex. While I knew I wanted far more than that, I was willing to take all I could get out of this.

At the shake of my head, he was quiet, his eyes searching mine.

"Okay then. Let's go," he said softly.

My body yearned for him the moment he stepped away, but I knew what I wanted, and it wasn't going to happen here in the icy cold in the middle of downtown Haven's Bay. So I let him lead me away. Everything he did made me feel taken care of in a way I hadn't felt before. He was a gentleman, he always had been. He opened the passenger door and made sure I was situated inside before closing the door. Then we were driving home, his headlights guiding the way through the dark night. I was hot all over, restless with need.

We were back to the house and inside within minutes. He hung his jacket, quickly adjusted the heat and started flicking on lights. I threw my coat off, kicked off my boots and walked across the room to him. I was impatient and restless, my emotions a tornado inside. Oddly enough, seeing Matthew had let the gates down inside. I'd been letting myself be emotionally and sexually half alive for too long. I felt so alive now, my skin prickling all over and need roaring through me.

I reached Dallas as he passed through the archway into the dining room, nudging the light switch on with his elbow. I caught his arm, and he spun back, opening his mouth to say something. Whatever he meant to say, he stopped when he saw the look on my face. I tugged him to me, sliding a hand up around the back of his neck and pulling him down. The moment our lips met, our kiss exploded. He didn't hesitate as I'd feared he would. He tangled a hand roughly in my hair, the other sliding down my back and pulling me tight against him.

I moaned at the feel of his cock hard against me. He kissed me as if I was the very air he needed to breathe. I wanted to let myself go up into flames with him. Somewhere along the way, I tore my mouth free, gulping in air. He yanked at my sweater, tossing it aside with my bra quick to follow.

He shoved my jeans and panties down, and I kicked them free. His fingers delved into my folds. "Fuck Audrey, you're so wet."

Restless and drenched with need, I frantically shoved his shirt up. I gasped as his teeth sank into the side of my neck, hot shivers racing through me. Inside of a second, I was moaning at the feel of his hands cupping my breasts and teasing my nipples. He rolled one between his thumb and forefinger, laving the other with his tongue. I savored the scrape of his stubble on the sensitive skin there, the soft bite of his teeth when they closed down around one of my nipples.

I was near frantic, yanking at his jeans,

curling my palm around the hard, hot length of his cock. He lifted his head.

"Fuck, Audrey. What you do to me," he growled.

"What do I do to you?"

I looked up to see his dark gaze on me, his eyes so hot I felt the burn of them. He stared at me, the air around us heavy. After a moment, he sifted his fingers through my hair.

"I want you. That's all. Just you," he murmured, his voice like a caress on my skin.

I'm not sure what I'd expected him to say. His words hit me, right in the heart. I shifted my legs restlessly, attempting to relieve the ache between my thighs. I pushed him back as I knelt in front of him, shoving his jeans down around his hips. His cock sprang free. I curled my palm around it, dragging my tongue along the bottom up to the tip, savoring the salty tang of the drop of pre-cum there. He tightened his hand in my hair and muttered my name roughly.

I swiped my tongue along his cock again. When I got to the head, I drew it into my mouth, all the way.

"Fuck, Audrey," he growled, his grip in my hair rough, the sting on my scalp a relief. "Let me..."

Whatever he meant to say was lost in a rough groan as I set to sucking on his cock. My wet grip slid up and down his length with my mouth. His cock hardened further under my touch. I savored every muttered curse, every time he said my name as if it was a curse and a prayer. I felt his balls tightening when I cupped them. I wanted to make him come right now, but suddenly he moved, yanking at my hair and lifting me swiftly.

"I'm not..."

"I know you're not done," he cut in "but that's not how this is ending, not tonight."

Inside of a few seconds, he stripped me bare and was lifting me onto the dining room table. He leaned forward, swiping his arm across the surface, knocking papers and file folders from his work onto the floor. The wood surface was cool on my back—the contrast to the heat of my body notching the wildness inside even further up. I looked up at him. My mouth went dry. He was so hot it was ridiculous. His chest was all muscle. My eyes were drawn to the corded muscles of his arms as he grabbed my hips and dragged me to the edge of the table. His jeans were hanging open, his cock wet from my mouth.

All of a sudden, his eyes widened slightly and he started to step back.

"Where are you going?" I asked, near frantic.

"Condom," he bit out. "I don't have one on me. I have to go check my luggage upstairs."

I shook my head. "Forget it. I'm clean, and I'm on the pill. I have been for years. I can't imagine you're anything other than clean. You're always prepared."

Dallas stared at me, his eyes dark, his expression unreadable. I started to have doubts. I'd been so lost in sensation I wasn't thinking through how my comment might've been interpreted.

"It's okay. I probably shouldn't have said that. If you want..."

He shook his head sharply. "Oh no. I want. Trust me, I want," he said bluntly.

Then, he was stepping back between the cage of my legs. He gripped his cock in his fist and dragged it through my folds. I almost came right then. The sensation was so sharp when his hard cock passed over my clit.

"Dallas please..."

Chapter Eleven

DALLAS

"Dallas please..." Audrey said, her words coming out on a low moan.

Sweet hell. She was so fucking gorgeous, so glorious. Her breasts were round and full, the nipples pink and taut, still damp from my attentions. Her hair almost matched the dark mahogany of the table. She was like a meal spread out for me. For a moment, I considered tasting her, but she was too impatient. She curled her legs around my hips and muttered my name again. I coated my cock in her juices. She was so wet, the insides of her thighs were damp. I gripped her hips, dragging her closer to the edge of the table.

"Audrey."

When I said her name, her eyes opened.

She rolled her hips into me when I dragged my cock through her folds once more. I couldn't wait anymore and positioned myself at her entrance. In one swift surge, I sank inside, straight to the hilt. She was so tight, so wet, made for me. She cried out, her channel clenching around me. I stared down at her. Our eyes locked together.

The feeling of being bare inside of her was so intense, I was at the edge instantly. Audrey felt so good, wet and pulsing around me. When I started to move, her hips arched up into every stroke. The sounds she made nearly made me lose control—soft, breathy pants and moans. Before I knew it, I was pounding into her, my fingers digging into her hips as I held on tight. I felt when she began to let go, her sex convulsing around me, her body going taut. She arched up on a loud cry, murmuring my name. I followed her over the edge, heat twisting at the base of my spine and then shooting through me as I spent myself inside of her. I stood there, buried deep inside of her, my head bowed as I tried to catch my breath.

After a moment, I managed to open my eyes. I didn't want this moment to end, so I leaned over and lifted her up against me, still inside of her. I carried her upstairs, leaving behind the disarray of our clothes on the floor. I didn't pull out of her until we were in the bathroom and even then I didn't want to. I drew back to turn on the hot water and nudged her into the shower, while I dragged my jeans off before joining her.

———

I woke at some point during the night when my phone buzzed on the night table beside me. I was accustomed to calls at all hours. My job demanded it. I lifted my phone reluctantly. Audrey was tangled up beside me, one of her legs thrown over mine, and her head tucked against my shoulder. I hoped the phone didn't wake her. I glanced at the screen and saw that it was one of the lead detectives on a major investigation, Cole Hanson. I let it go to voicemail and then pulled up my text screen.

What's up? Not a great time for a call.

Right. It's the middle of the night, but you usually answer anyway. We got a solid lead on the trafficking case.

I rolled my head to look at Audrey, sifting my hand through her hair, the silky locks sliding through my fingers. I texted with one thumb.

Keep me posted.

That's it?

I knew he was puzzled that I wasn't picking up the phone to call, but I didn't care to explain.

That's it. I'll call tomorrow.

Normally, I would call and want more information, but I couldn't bear to untangle myself from Audrey. It took me a while to fall back asleep, if only because my mind was spinning over Audrey. She'd teased me in the shower that she was going get every inch of me she could. She seemed to think my limit on sex only was amusing. I didn't know what to do about it. I wanted far more than sex with her. She made me want so much, I couldn't help but wonder if I was half crazy to let this go any further. Yet, I knew I couldn't stop it. Not now. I finally managed to fall asleep, if only because she was warm and soft against me.

AUDREY

The following morning, I sat at the dining room table, which had become the de facto office for Dallas and me. Sipping coffee, I was busy emailing back-and-forth with my lawyer about the itemized list I intended to have her send to Matthew. Canceling a wedding was a pain in the ass, in case you were wondering. The only factor working in my favor was that the scheduled date was over six months away. I felt lucky to be able to get refunds on anything. I had no option but to forfeit deposits. I was relieved I had a good job that paid well. After I graduated from NYU with my law degree, I'd taken a position as an Assistant Attorney General for New York State. I was a small fry compared to the lawyers working in the private sector, but I still made decent money.

The abrupt end of my engagement to Matthew had created a domino effect in my life. I'd only remained in New York because of my relationship with Matthew. I'd never intended to stay beyond graduation. New York was an amazing city—fun, buzzing with energy, and alive with so many options. It was easy to feel as if the world was at your fingertips there. Yet, for me, it was a fun place to live temporarily, or to visit. Matthew had persuaded me to stay, insisting we'd never get the career opportunities we had there anywhere else.

I looked around my family's home. I contemplated whether I could ask my parents if I could stay here for a while. While I loved it here, that didn't quite appeal to me either. Haven's Bay would always be a touchstone for me, but I couldn't quite imagine being here all the time. My mind spun to Dallas. I was practically chanting a mantra in my mind about him, reminding myself again and again that I shouldn't hope for more. Last night had been pure heaven. I could seriously get used to falling asleep tangled up beside him.

Dallas had been in and out of the dining

room this morning, alternating between working on his computer and taking calls in another room. It was clear he was handling something intense related to work. Although I supposed everything related to his work was intense. I didn't know much about what he did beyond the broad strokes. I knew from Thea he had been promoted quickly within the FBI, and he led a number of investigations out of the FBI's Boston office. Even she didn't know the details related to them because he couldn't talk about them. Sadly, I knew quite well that he'd been the investigator to stumble onto his father's financial crimes. He'd removed himself from the case, yet he still had to witness his family get torn apart over it.

He looked worried, his gaze tense today. It made my heart ache a little, if only because I didn't like seeing him like that. Thinking about him made me restless, so I went to the kitchen to start a fresh pot of coffee, needing something to keep me occupied. While it was brewing, I walked upstairs to drag the Christmas decorations out of the attic. I might be crazy, but since I was here and Christmas was right around the corner, I wanted to decorate the house.

I was halfway through stringing lights

around the fireplace when there was a knock at the front door. I heard Dallas' footsteps, and he leaned in the archway into the living room, his eyes widening when he saw what I was doing.

"What are you doing?" he asked.

"Hanging Christmas lights," I said, stating the rather obvious fact.

I knew his question wasn't about that, but more about why I would even be doing this. Yet, I didn't feel like answering because it meant contemplating the state of my heart.

He was quiet, something flashing in his eyes. "Okay, I'll get the door then."

He stepped into the entryway and opened the door. Cold air swirled inside. I heard a voice I recognized.

"Come on in, Howard," Dallas said.

I plugged in the lights around the fireplace, wiped my hands on my jeans and walked over to the entryway. "Hey, Howard. Long time no see," I said.

His eyes widened, a grin splitting his face. "Audrey! I heard from Sherry you were here. Good to see you."

"What brings you here, Howard?" Dallas asked.

"I thought I'd stop by to see if you'd seen anybody next door," Howard explained.

I angled my head to the side. "Why are you asking? We can't really see the house from here with the trees in between."

"I know, but since there's only a few houses nearby with anyone around, I'm checking. Someone broke in last night," he explained with a slow shake of his head.

"You've got to be fucking kidding me," Dallas said.

Howard sighed. "Honestly, I'm dealing with a break-in once or twice a week. Someone's got an organization going on around here. They're making bank too. They steal electronics and valuables from every house. When people give me estimates of what's missing, it's ten grand plus. They've even stolen vehicles from people that leave summer vehicles here. It surprised me somebody broke in nearby last night because I knew Dallas was here. They've mostly been breaking into homes that are surrounded by other vacation homes, so no one's even within a mile."

"How about I get you some coffee?" I asked as I stepped past the front door. "We can sit down for a few minutes."

I went into the kitchen to pour coffee, while Howard and Dallas sat down at the dining room table. When I returned, I could tell Dallas was in investigator mode. He had a notepad out and was jotting down dates and actually drawing a map. Leave it to him to go right to the details. By the time Howard was ready to go, Dallas had full accounting of whose home had been broken into, when and what was missing.

As Howard stood to leave, he caught Dallas' eyes. "Damn smart of Warren to ask you to check on this place. If anything, you being here will be the only reason this place doesn't get robbed too." Howard's gaze flicked between us. "How long will you two be around?"

I felt Dallas' eyes on me, but I didn't look his way. Anxiety bloomed in my chest. This shouldn't have felt like a loaded question, but it did.

Dallas spoke first. "I told Warren I'd be here until after the New Year."

I couldn't quite bring myself to answer because I didn't have an answer. What I wanted to say was I'd be here for the month too. That had been my plan before I encountered Dallas. I'd wanted the peace and quiet this place could offer me. Now, I wanted to soak every drop of time I could with Dallas. Yet, warning bells were ringing loudly in my mind. The more time I spent with him, the more I wanted him. That was dangerous.

Howard carried on after Dallas answered, asking him a few more questions and leaving me off the hook to discuss my plans. We saw Howard out, and I finished putting up the lights in the living room, while Dallas returned to his 'office' in the dining room.

Not much later, I slipped into a chair across from him. He appeared to be going back and forth between the map he'd penciled for the locations of the break-ins and something on his computer.

"I can't believe this," I said when he glanced up.

He shrugged. "I can. It's not like it hasn't happened here before. It's smart and easy pickings for somebody who just wants to make some quick cash."

"Seriously? How much money can they be making?"

Dallas cocked his head to the side, his mouth curling up at one corner. My belly did a little flip at that. His smiles were too delicious for me.

"You don't think like a criminal. It might not seem like much, but if they're pulling 10K value for every break in, they pawn it off and keep the cash. These guys are headed to one of the cities, Portland or Boston probably, and selling what they steal. I'm sure they have an arrangement in place with some pawn shops. I figured I would take notes and maybe I can be a little help while I'm here," he explained.

I nodded and took a sip of my freshly filled cup of coffee. "I'm sure Howard will appreciate it. You seem busy today. Is everything okay with work?" I asked.

He eyed me, his gaze assessing. "Nothing unusual. Some activity on a case I'm handling in Boston. You don't mind, do you?"

"No, of course not. It's your job. It's not like you expected me to be here. You certainly don't need to do anything different because I am."

As soon as I spoke, a thread of tension ran through me. I realized this was the point where he probably expected me to tell him what my plans were. The truth was, I wanted to stay here for the entire time that I would've been in Italy. That had been my original plan. I didn't want to go back to New York. That was the last place I wanted to be. Even though it would be nice to see my family, I wasn't up for anyone feeling bad for me about how things ended with Matthew. I preferred to stay here and lose myself in Dallas. Even though I knew it was a potentially disastrous idea, I'd patch up my heart and face the world later.

Chapter Thirteen

DALLAS

"Cole, do you think I need to come down there?" I asked, running a hand through my hair and spinning to look out the dining room windows. Audrey had gone outside to gather some balsam fir to make a wreath. Her bright red coat stood out against the snow as she walked through the trees at the edge of the yard, gathering branches that had fallen to the ground. I laughed to myself. Of course she wouldn't cut the branches. That wasn't her style.

Cole interrupted my train of thought. That's how easily distracted I was with Audrey. I prided myself on staying focused, and all it took was a gap between sentences and my mind spun to her like a weather vane in the wind.

"You don't have to come down, but it would probably help if you did," Cole replied. "We'll have him here for questioning by tonight. I can handle it, but if you were here, obviously you would handle the interview."

My eyes tracked Audrey's progress through the trees. I gave myself a shake, bringing my attention back to the phone call.

"Dallas?" Cole said.

I realized I'd waited a little too long before replying when he spoke. "You know what? I'll be there. I'll probably come down for tonight, do the interview and maybe stay through tomorrow, or the day after. Sound like a plan?"

"Of course."

He paused, and I sensed he wanted to ask me something. He cleared his throat.

"You doing okay?" he finally asked.

"Yeah. Of course. Why do you ask?"

"It's not that I don't think you deserve a vacation, but normally I would've expected you to already be on your way to Boston after our call this morning," he explained.

"Just taking care of a few things up here. I was actually helping the chief of police review details on the run of break-ins they've had here. That's the reason I'm up here to check on the house. But you're right. Normally, I would already be there. I'm testing myself to see if I can handle a vacation," I said with a little laugh.

Cole accepted my explanation, and we ended the call. I set the phone down on the table and spun back to watch Audrey in the yard. She had a small armful of balsam boughs now, definitely enough for a wreath. As she returned and walked back towards the house, the wind blew her hair in a wild swirl. My heart twisted in my chest. Cole was exactly right. Usually I would've been in Boston already. Hell, normally I'd have taken his call in the middle of the night and left right then.

I had a convenient excuse with Howard showing up today, but the truth was the only reason I wasn't already in Boston was because of Audrey. It made no fucking sense what I was doing. I'd given into need and longing, trying to convince myself that's all it was, and it would be enough. Stupidest thing I'd ever done. I gave myself a hard mental shake. It would probably be best for me to go to Boston. Probably best to stay more than a day or two. With Audrey here, the superficial reason of staying to keep an eye on the house was no longer necessary. I could let Warren know I had to leave for work, and I knew he wouldn't mind. There was a whole host of other things to consider. For example, he would then be worried about Audrey being here alone. They would probably want her to come visit with them.

I didn't know how she felt about that, but I sensed she didn't want to and for good reason. Hell, if I were her, I wouldn't either. She would be explaining things, trying to convince people not to feel bad, and trying to put a good spin on it. Separate from my own feelings, and I had somehow convinced myself I was separating them from this equation, it appeared she was relieved to have things over with Matthew. It appeared she wasn't too hurt beyond having her pride stung due to the betrayal. He'd clearly hurt her, but it was obvious she hadn't loved him.

For that, I was relieved. If she had, I probably would've punched him the other night. As it was, it had been entirely unnecessary. Audrey had stood up for herself and hadn't hesitated to hold her ground. She'd been glorious. I loved that feisty side of her. Damn. I was so fucked. It wasn't just lust, and I knew it. I spun away from the window when I saw her getting closer to the house, immediately sitting down in front of my computer and zapping off a few emails.

The investigation Cole had called about was a big one. They'd arrested one of our main targets in Connecticut and were bringing him up to Boston tonight. It was the biggest break we'd had thus far. My specialty was financial crimes, and this investigation had started there. The trail of money had led us to a massive human trafficking operation that ran out of Boston and New York. I wanted the chance to interview this guy. I had confidence in Cole though and had no doubt he could handle it as well as me. I was questioning leaving because Audrey was here. Which was all the more reason why I needed to go. I needed to draw that line for myself, as well as for her.

Cold air swirled in from the entryway as she entered. The front door sat in the center of the house with archways on either side, one leading to the living room and the other to the dining room and kitchen. I heard her kicking the snow off of her boots and then she stepped into the archway. Her cheeks were rosy, her lips pink, and her eyes bright. She was fucking gorgeous. She held up the cluster of balsam boughs.

"Just enough for a wreath. I didn't have to cut anything," she announced with a grin.

I managed to smile. I didn't know what it was about her decorating, but it made me feel strange. It made me want things I wasn't supposed to want. My job occupied most of my life in Boston. There would be no way that I could have the kind of life Audrey wanted and deserved. Even if I convinced myself I could, she'd be watching me work late nights and take off at odd hours during investigations.

It wouldn't hurt you to work less.

Shut up.

Audrey's a grown woman and plenty strong. She can make her own choice. You shouldn't make it for her.

Shut up.

Great internal debate. I held her gaze and smiled, though it hurt a little. "So you did. Will that go on the front door?"

She nodded, glancing down to shake some of the snow from the boughs onto the tile floor.

I considered that I should tell her now I would be going to Boston for a few days, but I didn't. I watched her walk off into the back porch behind the kitchen where she got to work weaving the wreath together. I went upstairs to pack. I heard her footsteps come up the stairs and stop in the doorway into the guest bedroom.

"Where are you going?" she asked.

I zipped my bag closed and spun to look at her, keeping my expression calm. "They made an arrest in Connecticut for an investigation I've been handling. I need to go to Boston tonight for interviews."

She was quiet for a beat, while my heart twisted in my chest. "Okay, drive safe."

I didn't know what I'd expected, but a small part of me had wanted her to argue the point. Hell, I wanted her to go with me. I didn't say anything and simply nodded, swallowing against the tight feeling in my throat. Her eyes had gone from open to guarded. I hated it. But this was completely necessary. She didn't need to think I could be someone who I wasn't. I loved my job, and I was damn good at it. I couldn't consider giving it up for something domestic like love. I almost flinched internally when that word passed through my mind.

"Do you need me to make some coffee for you to go?" she asked as she turned and walked back down the hallway.

She was always so polite. Of course, she

would offer to do that, and it made it all the harder to leave.

"Sure," I said quickly, snagging my bag and following her down the stairs.

I jogged outside to start my car, returning to find her prepping a pot of coffee. We waited in silence while the coffee brewed. If she was upset, I couldn't feel it. She'd walled herself off from me. I could feel the distance she created acutely. I hated that too. I hated all of this. I wanted to step to her, run my hands through her hair, cup her cheeks, and kiss her. I wanted to tell her I would be back tonight. Because for her, I would make the four hour drive to Boston and back in the same day, if only so I could fall asleep beside her again.

I didn't do any of that. She filled a thermos and handed it to me.

"Will you text me when you get there? The roads are icy," she said conversationally. "When do you think you'll be back?"

I hesitated, staring into the layers of her eyes, the swirl of colors in the depths. I saw a hint of hurt, but she was too proud to let it show. I'd made my limits clear, and she would respect them. Even though right now, I wished like hell she wouldn't.

"Either tomorrow or the day after," I finally said. "I should know tonight."

She simply nodded and saw me to the door. For a flash, I considered kissing her, but I didn't. I turned, walked to my car and drove away.

Chapter Fourteen

AUDREY

"Dammit, dammit, dammit," I said to no one.

Because no one was here but me. I was in this fucking house alone, which was exactly what I'd thought I wanted when I drove up here a few days ago. But that was before I saw Dallas, that was before I let myself tumble into this madness with him. That was before I'd realized with painful clarity what a hold he still had on my heart, my body, my soul, and my mind. Sweet hell. I could not keep him out of my thoughts. I'd gone on a crazy cleaning spree the following afternoon after he left. My parents usually spent a month or two here in the summer and often came up every few months in between to check on things, maybe stay for a long weekend. The house didn't get regular cleanings, so I'd gone nuts. I'd cleaned all of the bathrooms and the kitchen. I'd swept, vacuumed and mopped. I'd been restless and needed something to burn off my energy.

I was filthy by the time it was over, so I took a quick shower and pulled on my most comfortable pair of fleece sweatpants and a fleece sweatshirt. I settled into the living room couch with a blanket and a cup of hot cocoa, intending to lose myself in silly television. I was deep into a ridiculous reality show when I heard a sound in the background. I couldn't figure out what it was, but it kept up. I finally turned off the TV and listened. It sounded like a dog whining. I walked to the back door off of the kitchen porch to find said dog shivering in the cold by the door.

The dog was a medium-sized, golden colored dog. It didn't quite look like a golden retriever, but some sort of mix. I held my hand out, kneeling inside the door.

"Hey sweetie, did you want to come in?"

The dog eyed me cautiously, but made no move from its spot a few feet away. It let out another shivering whine. I left the porch door open and returned to the kitchen. I snagged a few pieces of sandwich meat, figuring if anything could bribe the little dog, maybe this would. Returning to the porch, I found the dog had sidled into the corner inside the porch. It was still shivering, but at least here it was out of the wind. I walked carefully to the porch door and closed it before kneeling down again. I held out my hand with the tempting sandwich meat and waited. After a brief standoff, the dog came over, sniffed my hand and took a cautious bite of the deli turkey. That's all it took and then it followed me right inside.

I loved dogs. That had been another point of contention between Matthew and I. He'd declared he didn't hate them, but he thought they were messy and not worth it. I should've known then he wasn't worth my time. I gave myself a shake. It didn't matter. Matthew and I were over. This was a new chapter for me, and this little stray had just showed up to take part. I allowed the dog to meander about downstairs while I looked through the pantry, wondering if we had any of the old canned food that we used to feed my last childhood dog, Bradley.

When I couldn't find any, I made some rice and chicken. Our vet had always said this was the best thing to start with when Bradley had an upset stomach. I figured I could safely feed this to the dog until I could go to the store tomorrow. The dog quickly came over when I set the food on the floor. While the dog was eating, I leaned over to ascertain whether this was a boy or a girl. Definitely a girl. I decided to call her Molly. After she finished eating, she cautiously approached me when I held my hand out. In short order, she seemed to decide I was safe.

I curled up on the couch and didn't even bother trying to keep her from climbing up there with me. Finding her made Dallas' absence less sharp. I was busy petting her and telling myself it was good Dallas had left. I needed to remember I was here to get my head on straight after everything with Matthew. I didn't need to dive right into something with anyone, much less Dallas. At least that's what I told myself.

My phone buzzed, and I picked it up to see a text from Dallas.

Letting you know I won't make it back until tomorrow at the earliest.

I stared at his text, my heart clenching. Dammit, why did this little tiny thing matter so much to me?

Thanks for letting me know.

I didn't expect him to reply, but then he did.

How are things there?

I stared at his question, wondering what to say. The true answer would be:

I miss you and wish you would come back.

But I couldn't say that. I stuck to the concrete.

I cleaned the house and found a dog.

?

I assume you're asking about the dog, not cleaning the house.

I could practically feel him laughing when I got the eye roll emoticon in return. *I heard a dog whining outside. No collar and pretty thin. So she's here now. I've named her Molly. When you come back, she'll be here. I hope everything's okay with your investigation.*

When he didn't reply, I set the phone down, thinking that was it.

A while later my phone buzzed again.

I miss you.

My heart went a little bit crazy.

Chapter Fifteen

DALLAS

I threw a file folder on the desk and plunked down in the chair across from Cole. Running a hand through my hair, I sighed.

"Well, I think we got as much as we could for now," I said.

Cole nodded. "Agreed. This guy's not ready to fold yet, but we'll get there. Right now, he's busy trying to keep himself out of trouble. You planning on staying through until tomorrow?"

I eyed him, considering his question. The easy answer would be yes. Yet, I was oddly distracted. The only time I hadn't been distracted was when I was in the interview room. Then my attention was laser focused. At all other times, Audrey kept dancing along the edges of my thoughts. I'd missed her like hell last night. Staring down into another night without her made me so uncomfortable, I shied away from thinking about it. I looked over at Cole.

"Dunno. Do you think it's necessary?"

Cole looked across at me, his dark gaze assessing. Cole knew me well. We'd worked together for years. I sensed he noticed something was off with me, but he stayed quiet.

"I don't think it's necessary. I'd say you probably still need that vacation," he finally replied.

"Why do you say that?" I asked, feeling slightly defensive.

I rolled my head from side to side, attempting to ease the tension bundled in my neck and shoulders.

"You seem a little off that's all. Everybody needs a break, so let yourself have one."

I nodded and stood, quickly striding to the corner in his office where there was a coffee pot. I poured myself a cup and took a sip. I spun back to look at him, holding the paper cup aloft. "I see you're still an expert at shitty coffee."

Cole flashed a grin and leaned back in his chair with a chuckle. "Gets the job done, and that's all that matters."

"That it does. All right, I'm gonna check on a few things in my office. I'll let you know later if I'm staying or going."

He nodded, his eyes already on his laptop on his desk. I returned to my office, quickly rifling through the stack of mail and files my receptionist had left on my desk. She'd been gone for the day before I'd gotten here. I'd arrived in Boston by six-thirty in the evening yesterday and worked until past midnight. It was now going on nine o'clock the following night. I glanced at the clock on the wall, considering what time I would arrive in Haven's Bay if I were to leave now—around one in the morning. I made a quick decision I would stay the night and head north in the morning.

I wasn't comfortable with how much I wanted to climb in my SUV, drive through the dark, cold night to curl up beside Audrey and sleep. As I was sitting at my desk going through a few more things, my phone rang. I glanced at the screen and saw it was Thea.

I answered quickly. "Hey Thea, what's up?"

"Not much. I was just checking in. How are things up in Maine?" she asked.

"They were fine when I left yesterday afternoon. I'm in Boston right now," I explained.

Thea's heavy sigh echoed through the speaker on my phone. "Seriously Dallas? You need a vacation."

"I know. I'm going back up tomorrow. We had a big arrest on a case, and I came down for the interview."

"You'll always be able to find a reason to go back to work, but it doesn't change the fact that you need a life outside of work."

Some variation of this conversation had happened with Thea many times. She worried about me. Most of the time I brushed it off. Just now, all it made me think of was Audrey.

"I know, I know. I promise I'll be back in Haven's Bay by tomorrow, and I promise I'll stay the rest of the month."

I could practically feel her eyes rolling through the phone when she spoke. "Yet, you promised you were going to stay for the month before, and you're already in Boston. It hasn't even been a week."

"Thea, cut me some slack, okay?"

"Fine," she muttered. "Anyway, how is Audrey? I'm worried about her."

"I think she's okay," I offered. "She says it's for the best."

Thea was quiet for a beat. "Yeah, I'm relieved it's over. I told her after the fact I suspected something was up. I wish I'd known what he was doing. I should've said something."

"Thea, what would you have told her?"

"I dunno, nothing I suppose. I didn't know anything until she found out," she said with a sigh.

"Thea, you didn't have anything to tell her. Stop feeling bad about it."

"I was trying to be supportive, but all along I didn't think he was the right guy for her. He just wasn't... I don't know. I didn't think he was good enough for her," she finally said.

I wholeheartedly agreed, but I wasn't about to get into all the reasons why with my little sister. If she knew what I'd been doing with Audrey the last two nights, she'd run me up one side and down the other. She was fiercely protective of her friends and Audrey was her best friend. My heart clenched, emotion tightening my throat. What the fuck was I doing? I needed to think about what was smart right now. I forced my attention to my call.

"I'll be back in Haven's Bay tomorrow. What are you plans for Christmas?" I asked, shifting gears away from Audrey.

"I don't know. I called Noah and told him

we should all go up and meet you in Haven's Bay. We could go to the house," she offered.

The holidays had been a loaded, rather depressing time for my family the last few years. With our mom passed away and our father in jail, it was just the four of us. While everyone understood why our father was sitting in jail, there were definitely some feelings about how it had all played out. Our family had splintered. Ian had been furious at me at first because he had a hard time believing our father had done what he did. When everything came out publicly, he'd accepted it, but he'd been pissed I hadn't shared more to begin with. He didn't quite grasp that I couldn't go around spilling investigation details like that. He'd argued that since I'd been taken off the case once I knew our father was involved, I should've told them more. It had been awkward to say the least.

Thea and I were the closest, probably because I was the quintessential overprotective older brother, and I had no problem admitting it. Noah had followed me into the FBI, so while he'd been no less devastated by our father's actions, he'd had a better understanding of why I had to stay quiet. Ian was busy trying to rebuild our family fortune again. I didn't give a damn about money. Money didn't make anybody happy. That much I knew. It made people greedy though. Once they had it, they often wanted more. That's exactly what had happened with our father.

"Dallas?" Thea asked.

I realized I'd been silent too long. "If you want to come up to Haven's Bay, that would be nice. Audrey would love it," I offered.

"Oh, is she staying through the holidays?"

"I'm not sure, but it sounds like she might. Can't say I blame her. I spoke to Warren. I think he'd love for her to come down there, but I'm guessing she'd rather not spend too much time dwelling on her canceled wedding."

Thea sighed again.

"You're about to set a record for sighing today," I said with a chuckle.

She sighed more dramatically this time. "Maybe I am. I just feel bad for what happened."

"Well, I think we'd all feel a lot worse if she ended up marrying that idiot."

My desk phone rang, so I wrapped up our call. Thea said she'd be in touch with our brothers and let me know their plans. After our call, I glanced around my office. It was quieter here at night, but there was still a low hum of activity. The FBI never closed. I gave myself a mental shake and tried to focus. I took care of a few things and then drove home to my apartment, letting myself into the quiet space. This was my usual routine— work, work, work, come home, sleep, work out in the morning and go back to work.

Tonight, my place felt lonely, if only because I missed Audrey. I fell asleep wondering if I'd been flat insane to let her know I missed her and contemplating just how it was she had such a powerful hold on me. I kept telling myself it didn't make sense I could feel this much in this short of a time. Yet, it wasn't as if I didn't know her. I'd known her forever. I tried to chalk it up to lust, but it was becoming more apparent it wasn't simply that.

Chapter Sixteen

AUDREY

It was dark when I woke and heard footsteps downstairs. Fear flashed through me. I suddenly recalled my car was in the garage and Dallas' SUV was gone from the driveway. From the outside, it would look as if no one were here. I lay still, my heart pounding frantically in my chest as I wondered who was in the house. My bedroom door was closed, and I contemplated whether I could get out of bed to tiptoe over and lock it without anyone hearing me. Molly had fallen asleep at the foot of my bed. She lifted her head and whined softly. I considered shushing her, but then I realized if I let her bark, she might chase away the intruder.

I stayed quiet, barely breathing with my

heart racing as I prayed whoever was here would stay downstairs and get whatever they wanted. There was a clatter and then Molly leapt off the bed and barked sharply. A few more barks, and I heard footsteps quickly making their way down the front hall and the door slamming shut.

I grabbed my phone. I should've dialed 911. Instead, the first thing I did was text Dallas.

I think someone just broke into the house.

As soon as I sent the text, I wondered what the hell I was doing. There wasn't anything he could do to help. He was in Boston, and I was here. Yet, my instinct had been to reach out to him because somehow he made me feel safe. I stood and carefully looked out the front window. I could see taillights receding in the darkness down the driveway. I quickly dialed 911, reporting the burglary and letting them know the car was taking a left on the road. The other line rang as I was finishing my call. I glanced at the screen to see Dallas's name flash.

I wished I could undo the text I'd sent. I contemplated whether or not I should answer and then realized it would seem ridiculous if I didn't. I'd just texted him, so it was obvious I was awake.

"Hello," I answered.

"Are you okay?" he asked quickly.

"I've already called 911. I'm fine. I shouldn't have texted you."

"What happened?" His voice was low and taut. He sounded almost angry.

"I woke up because I heard footsteps downstairs," I explained.

"And?" he asked, prompting me to continue.

"Molly barked and whoever was here left."

"Molly?"

"The dog I texted you about last night."

As I spoke, she sidled against me, and I stroked her head.

"Oh right. Well, thank God for Molly. What happened after they left?"

"They took a left on the road, which I just told the police. The police said they're on their way here."

"I'm driving up there now."

"Dallas, that's ridiculous. It's three in the morning."

"Don't argue with me about this, Audrey. I'll be there."

The line went dead. I stared at my phone. It was absolutely pointless for him to drive four hours right now. I quickly texted him.

There's no need for you to drive here in the middle of the night. The police are already on their way.

I'll be there soon.

I turned and sank down onto the edge of my bed. It shouldn't have felt so good to know he was coming, but it did. I missed him, and it made no sense. How could I care so much in such a short period of time? With a mental shake, I stood and dragged on a pair of fleece pants. I needed to be halfway decent for when the police arrived.

———

I padded through the kitchen the following morning, starting coffee and checking the fridge for what I might want for breakfast. After my unexpected awakening, the police had stopped by and done a quick check to make sure everything was safe. Whoever had broken in had punched through the window by the kitchen door and unlocked the door that way. I wondered if the sound of breaking glass might've been what originally nudged me out of my sleep. The police had done a walk-through to find nothing missing and assured me they would be patrolling the road for the rest of the night. I barely slept after that. Frankly, I wouldn't have slept at all if it hadn't been for Molly. Her presence was a comfort.

She was following me around like a new shadow. Her fur was ragged and dull, and she was too thin with her ribs and her hipbones showing. It hurt my heart. I wondered where she'd come from. I'd asked the police last night. None of them had seen her before, and one of them made a passing comment that she might've been a puppy somebody got over the summer and then left behind. She didn't look that old. It was hard to know with her so underweight. When 9 o'clock rolled around, I planned to call the local vet and bring her in as soon as I could.

Meanwhile, I made her more chicken and rice, intending to go to the grocery store today to stock up on dog food. The coffee maker beeped just as there was a sharp knock at the front door. Molly let out a bark and ran to the door. My heart jumped. I couldn't help but wish for Dallas to arrive. My feelings were all a muddle inside. Dear God. Talk about confused. I had feelings about my feelings.

On the one hand, I wanted Dallas here because I didn't quite feel safe staying here alone after last night. I also missed him like crazy, and I didn't know what to do with how fast I was falling for him. In my fitful hours after the break-in last night, I'd had many a conversation with myself about how ridiculous it was to think I was falling for him. I might've lusted after him for years, but that didn't explain the emotional intensity I felt when I was with him.

I wondered what Thea would think if she knew what had happened. She would probably tell me I was setting myself up for heartbreak. I'd heard her bemoan Dallas' lack of a social life for years. She worried about him and thought he worked too much. I walked to the door, slid the bolt free and swung it open. Cold air rushed in. Dallas stood there, his dark hair rumpled and his eyes weary. His gaze swept over me, breaking away when Molly barked again.

Dallas knelt down and held his hand out. "You must be the girl who scared the bad guy away last night," he said softly.

Molly leaned forward, carefully sniffing his hand before sidling up to him. He stroked her head and murmured something.

I tried to tamp my emotions down. My reaction was ridiculous. For God's sake, he was simply being kind to a dog. Matthew's dislike of dogs had bothered me. Dallas stood slowly after one last stroke for Molly. Seeing how weary he was made my heart clench. I stepped back, gesturing for him to come in. He toed his boots off, hung his jacket and tossed his bag on the floor. I led the way into the kitchen with Molly following us.

"Come on. I have coffee ready. I can't believe you drove all the way up here in the middle of the night. You really didn't need to," I said as I poured him a cup of coffee.

He slipped into a chair at the table and ran a hand through his rumpled hair. He eyed me, his rich blue gaze searing me. His jaw was tight, and he looked tense all over. My chest knotted with emotion. I didn't like seeing him this way. I handed him his coffee and sat down across from him. He took a gulp of coffee and then sighed.

"So what did the police say last night?"

I quickly summarized.

"Any word yet if they ID'd the car?"

"No. I didn't have a car description because it was dark."

He nodded tightly. "Okay, I'll go talk to Howard today."

I didn't particularly want to dwell on last night. Thinking about it made me anxious, and I was relieved everything was okay. My attention swung to him. "How did everything go in Boston?"

"As well as could be expected," he replied before taking another gulp of coffee.

I wanted to ask more questions, but I reminded myself he didn't have the kind of job he could talk much about. I took another sip of coffee and leaned back in my chair.

"So you're staying through Christmas?" he asked abruptly.

I stared at him for a long moment and then finally nodded. I supposed when I started hanging Christmas lights, my actions had cemented my plans. That's what I had planned to do before I knew he was here anyway.

"I think so. If you need to go back to Boston, you should. Seeing as I'm here..."

He shook his head sharply. "No, I'm sticking with my plan. I was asking because Thea wants to come up and persuade Noah and Ian to join us too."

"That would be fun," I said. "I'll call her later today."

Dallas drained his coffee and stood abruptly, striding to the sink and setting his empty mug beside it. "I could use a shower," he said before spinning and walking out of the room.

I didn't know what to make of the way he felt. He was tense and seemed irritated. I spun my phone around on the table, pulling up the text he'd sent the other night before I'd texted him about the break in.

I miss you.

I wondered why he'd said that. It didn't seem like he wanted to be back here, most especially not around me. I felt Molly's warm presence rub against my leg and looked down at her, stroking my palm over her head.

"Hey sweetie. That was Dallas. He loves dogs," I explained.

Her warm brown eyes held mine as if though she somehow understood what I was saying.

Chapter Seventeen

DALLAS

I shook the snow off of my jacket as I stepped into the police station. I looked ahead to find a familiar face. Patsy Johnson had been the receptionist here as long as I could remember. Her once dark hair was streaked with gray, but her blue eyes were still bright. She flashed a smile when she saw me.

"Dallas! I thought you might be in to see Howard today. He said he had a call from you. So good to see you."

"Always good to see you, Patsy. How are you?"

"Good, good. I have three grandkids now. I bet..." She paused, her mouth twisting with a sad smile. "I'm sorry. I was about to say your mother would love for you to have grandkids, but she's not here to see them."

"It's okay, Patsy. She'd have been crazy for grandkids."

This would usually be the point when we checked in about family, but Patsy was one of many locals my father had fleeced. She'd gone out of her way to let me know I didn't need to feel bad for my father's actions, but it was still an awkward point for me.

"Howard available?" I asked, skipping past the moment.

"Of course."

She tapped a button on her desk, buzzing the door to the back open for me. I stepped into the back hallway, recalling the only time I'd actually been in the back of the police station was when I'd shown up to bail my youngest brother, Ian, out of a bit of trouble. He'd been sixteen and got caught drag racing on a vacant road with his friends outside of town. He'd always been the wildest of us. He'd turned that energy toward work these days and for that I was relieved.

I heard Howard call my name and followed the sound of his voice into a doorway.

"Good to see you, Dallas. How the hell did you get back to Haven's Bay so fast?" he asked, waving me to a chair across from his desk.

I shrugged as I sat down. "Hit the road early this morning," I replied, leaving out the fact I'd left within minutes of Audrey's text. "Damn glad Audrey found that stray dog yesterday. Sounds like the dog barking sent whoever was there running."

I shifted my shoulders, trying to ease the tension there. To say I'd been tense for hours was an understatement. I'd been sleeping restlessly before I got Audrey's text because I should've just driven up here earlier. That was what I'd wanted to do. After her text and our quick call, I'd thrown on my clothes, grabbed my bag and left.

Howard leaned back in his chair with a sigh. "That's what the guys told me this morning. She doin' okay?"

"Oh yeah. She says she's fine. A bit rattled and freaked out, but okay."

My words sounded calm, but my tone belied the fierce concern I felt. It had taken an act of will to leave the house after I arrived this morning. I didn't want to leave her alone, but she'd announced she was taking Molly to the vet and had some errands to do.

"Where the hell did she find that dog anyway?" Howard asked.

"Showed up whining at the back of the house. She's already named her Molly. She's a sweetie, definitely a keeper, but not much more than a skeleton with fur. Audrey'll spoil her rotten," I said with a chuckle.

"Oh, I bet she will. Wanna take a look at what we've got from the different reports?" Howard asked, his gaze sobering.

I left Howard's office later after we'd pored over the various burglary reports. Howard had a few leads. As much as I wanted to take over the whole damn investigation from him, I had absolutely no jurisdiction. It was small-town, petty burglary. Yet, it felt urgent because of what had happened last night and the fact it involved Audrey's safety.

I couldn't shake myself out of the emotional confusion she elicited. It was bothering me that I'd missed her. I'd only been away from her for two nights. It shouldn't have gotten to me that much. Hell, I knew I wanted her like mad. But wanting wasn't the same as what I felt now. I'd felt almost visceral pain when I was concerned about her last night.

I gave myself a shake and hopped in my SUV. As I was driving past Emile's, I saw Russ Porter stepping out of his truck. I spun into the parking lot and rolled my window down.

"Russ!"

Russ glanced over, his face cracking with a smile when he saw me.

"Dallas! Long time, no see," he commented as I rolled to a stop beside his truck.

Russ was an old friend. We'd graduated from high school around the same time and attended college together. I'd gone on into FBI training, while he'd gone into his family's business. I climbed out, and he pulled me in for a quick hug before leaning against my car.

"Didn't expect to see you around," he commented.

My visits to Haven's Bay had dwindled after everything went down with my father. We used to get together every summer for fishing.

"Yeah, don't get here as often as I'd like. Warren asked me to check on their place, and I needed a break from work. I'm here for the month."

"Wanna grab a beer together?" he asked, nudging his chin toward Emile's.

"Sure."

We turned in unison and walked into Emile's. I was at loose ends and out of sorts. It would be good to catch up with Russ and maybe it would take my mind off of Audrey. We settled into a table in the back corner. Emile's was a regular hang out for locals. Open year-round, it functioned as a combination coffee shop, deli and bar. Yet another place owned by Sherry and Emile. Emile caught my eyes from behind the bar, flashing a grin.

He rounded the bar and came over to the table. "Sherry mentioned you and Audrey were around."

The three of us chatted for a few minutes about the weather and summer fishing. Emile waved one of the staff over with two beers for us. Before he stepped away, he glanced back. "How long will you be here?" he asked.

"At least until after the New Year."

"Damn good to have you around. Make sure to stop by again," he said.

I glanced to Russ. He must've sensed the slight confusion in my expression.

"What? Dude, you grew up here. Of course people miss you. Everyone knows you had nothing to do with the shit your dad pulled. Since you won't come out and say it, I will. You've been avoiding this place ever since that shit went down. No need. Be good to see you in the summer again too."

I rolled my head from side to side, easing

the sudden tension building in my shoulders. All I had to do was think about my dad and what he'd done to get tense. I took a gulp of my beer.

"It's hard to come here and look at everybody he betrayed," I finally said.

Russ ran a hand through his dark brown hair and nodded. "I bet, but it's not like you didn't do everything you could to clean up his mess."

I took a deep breath and let it out. "Right. I did what I could."

Russ was quiet for a beat, his dark gaze assessing. "How are Noah, Ian and Thea?" he asked.

"Pretty good. You might be seeing them soon too. Thea wants to round the boys up for Christmas."

Russ flashed a grin. "Leave it to Thea. She's always herding everyone up."

I chuckled. "That she is."

"Heard Audrey's big wedding is off. She planning on staying through the holidays too?"

Russ couldn't know that was a loaded question. The superficial reason for me to be here was no longer necessary. Not with Audrey here.

"Think so. Says she's not up for her

family feeling bad about her canceling the wedding. I'm not willing to leave her here alone either, not after what happened last night."

Russ arched a brow in question. I quickly explained about the attempted burglary.

He shook his head slowly. "Damn. Glad she's okay. Howard's been chasing his tail on that one. My guess?"

"What's your guess?"

"Couple of those kids just outside the edge of town. They're always looking for a quick buck to score drugs."

"Have you told Howard?" I asked.

"Yup. Stopped by a few weeks ago. One of the places they broke into was down the road from us."

"Any names?"

Russ continued, and I recognized a few names from my discussion earlier with Howard. I needed to leave this one alone. It was chafing at me, but Howard clearly had as good of a handle as I would. My anger wouldn't help. This had gone from a helpful interest to way too personal. All because it involved Audrey.

Conversation moved on. Russ filled me in on his life. He helped run his family's commercial fishing and timber business. Married with two kids, he was settled and happy to be so in Haven's Bay.

Somewhere along the way, conversation turned back to Audrey. "Okay if I let Julie know Audrey's around? She heard what happened, and she's all worried. How is Audrey holding up anyway?"

"I think she's okay. Fucking asshole screwed around on her with one of her friends."

Russ' eyes widened. "Jesus fucking Christ. Asshole is one way to put it. I guess she's better off without him."

"You're telling me. Yeah, she said things weren't great for a while and then this. Honestly, she says she's relieved. It's not a secret she's here, so feel free to tell Julie. I'm sure she'd love to catch up."

I wanted the conversation off of Audrey simply because talking about her made me think about her and thinking about her made me want her. Thinking about her also made me worry about what happened last night. More to the point, it made me worry about the depth of my response. I'd been in a near panic driving up last night. I didn't panic. Ever. I stayed calm no matter what. Yet, all bets were off when it came to Audrey.

I managed to get the topic off of Audrey,

only to have Russ zero right back in after he updated me on his kids.

"You ever gonna settle down?" he asked.

I shook my head slowly. "Not in the cards for me. My job's not really a good fit for family life."

"Why do you say that?"

"Dude, you know what I do. I deal with ugly shit. My hours are long and late, and I don't have a lot of spare time."

Russ rolled his eyes. "Dude, you forget I met one of your best buds from work. He's got kids, and he's doing the same damn thing. Might be good for you not to have your whole life be your work. I'm just saying."

I knew he had a point, yet considering that brought me face to face with an uncomfortable truth. There was only one woman I could imagine settling down with. *Audrey*. I simply didn't know if I could be the man she deserved.

I ran a hand through my hair with a sigh. "Maybe, maybe not. We'll see.

"You wanna know what I think?" he asked with a sly grin.

"Not really, but that never stopped you before."

He chuckled. "You used to have a thing for Audrey. That last summer you were both here, I thought you were gonna have a meltdown every time you saw her. I figured maybe you two would eventually find your way to each other, but then she got engaged. Now she's free again, maybe something will come of it."

My heart gave a swift kick. I couldn't fucking believe he'd zeroed in that fast on Audrey.

"Dude, she just broke up with her fiancé," I said.

"Dude, he was screwing around on her."

I managed to laugh off Russ' comment and departed Emile's not much later. Snow had started to fall softly. With the way the wind was blowing, I sensed a nor'easter was on its way. I swung by the grocery store to pick up some beer and wine. After I turned onto the coastal road leading toward Audrey's family home, I slowed as I drove past my childhood home. It was sitting vacant. I hadn't even been able to bring myself to stop by yet. Perhaps I should've worried about a break-in, although there was nothing to steal. The house was emptied except for the furniture. I still hadn't decided what to do about the home. Technically, it was mine, but it didn't feel right.

My heart gave another kick. Thinking

back to my conversation with Russ, he hit on something uncomfortable. Despite what my father had done, my family had been close before. Though our father had always been distant and cold, he'd loved our mother. She'd been his one and only soft spot. Our mother had been the center that held our family to-gether. Her death knocked away the anchor in his life. I shook my head as I paused in the road, looking down the winding driveway. I had so many reasons why I'd figured living a bachelor's life as an FBI agent was going to be my life forever.

Audrey whirling into my life like this was making me question a lot of things, all of them making me uncomfortable. After a last glance at the stark tree branches standing tall against the sky, I kept driving. The clouds were thickening out over the ocean. Snow was spitting here and there with the wind picking up.

I grinned when Molly met me at the door. After petting her, kicking off my boots and hanging my jacket, I headed straight for the kitchen, not wanting to ponder that I was damn happy to be here. Because Audrey was here. Whatever she was cooking smelled amazing. I stepped through the archway into the kitchen.

"Damn, smells good in here. What are you cooking?"

Audrey spun around. Her hair was up in a messy knot, loose tendrils falling around her face. Her cheeks were flushed, and she had a streak of something on her face. I grinned because she was so damn cute. Turning away, she quickly rinsed her hands in the sink.

"I'm making lasagna. I haven't made it in a while because Matthew was a health freak and wouldn't eat it. I decided I'll cook all of my favorite stuff while I'm here," she said over her shoulder.

I refrained from pointing out any guy who didn't like lasagna was surely an asshole. In his case, Matthew was turning out to be more of an idiot than I'd originally thought. Audrey loved to cook and was crazy good at it. Whenever she'd be at our house with Thea years back, she often cooked. I was already half falling for her back then. The whole time I kept telling myself I couldn't, but it was near impossible once she was old enough for me to stop making that excuse. She took the beer from my hand and put it in the fridge as I set the wine bottle on the counter.

"Be right back," she said.

I heard the bathroom door open and close in the hallway. When she returned, she looked over with a sheepish smile. "You could've told me I had sauce on my face," she said with a low laugh as she returned to assembling the lasagna at the counter.

I chuckled. "It looked good on you."

I sat down at the kitchen table, only to have Molly come over and rest her chin on my knee. "How did it go at the vet?"

Audrey's gaze flicked down to Molly with a soft smile. "The vet said she's in okay health, but she's underweight. As if we couldn't see that. The vet thinks she's about nine months old. She figures the police might be right, that somebody probably got her as a puppy this summer and then left her here. I can't believe somebody would do that," she said with a huff.

"It might not be as nefarious as you think. It could be that she ran off. I'm not saying that's okay," I offered.

Audrey glanced over at me and shrugged. "Maybe so. Anyway, she's had her first round of shots now. The vet gave me a special diet to give her to help her put the weight on gradually. She said it'll take four to six weeks before Molly gets to a normal weight and told me to be careful and not overfeed her."

"Are you planning to take Molly with you to New York?"

Audrey lifted the pan of lasagna and slid it into the oven. Turning, she met my gaze, her hazel eyes flashing. "I'm keeping her, so I'll figure it out," she said firmly.

"Let me know if you need any help," I said. "Speaking of help, if you need help moving out of your apartment with Matthew, just say so. We could go down whenever you want."

Her eyes widened. "You'd do that?"

"Of course. I figure he's not going to make it pleasant for you."

She stroked Molly's head when Molly padded over to her side. "No, he probably won't. It looks like it might snow tonight, so maybe once we have a few clear days. I'd rather take care of it before Christmas. By the way, Thea called. She's got Ian and Noah coming up for Christmas. She offered to help me move too. It was Matthew's apartment originally, so I don't have any furniture."

I nodded, my chest tightening again. I didn't like thinking about how Matthew had treated her. No matter how relieved I was on her behalf that she'd dumped him on his ass, just as he should've been, it pissed me off he'd screwed around on her.

Audrey brushed a loose lock of hair away from her face and curled her hands on the edge of the counter. She wore a fitted denim button-down shirt, the buttons pulled tight across her breasts. My cock was already hard and had been since the moment I'd seen her. She had this crazy effect on me. It was a wild mix of emotion and lust, the two feeding into each other and making me feel more out-of-control than I ever had in my life. Molly meandered out of the kitchen, and I heard her feet padding up the stairs. I caught Audrey's gaze.

"Where do you think she's going?"

Audrey grinned. "Oh she's already decided her favorite place to nap is on the foot of my bed. I don't mind. I bet she hasn't had anywhere warm to be for months, so she can sleep wherever she wants as far as I'm concerned."

She turned and set the timer on the oven and then pulled two wineglasses from the cabinet. Picking up the bottle of wine, she waved in the direction of the dining room. "Let's go in here."

This was an older home and had fireplaces in the dining room and the living room. I'd noticed she had a fire going in the dining room on my way to the kitchen. I slipped into a chair at the corner of the table. As she stepped to my side to pour the wine, her presence was so close I wanted to touch her. Next thing I knew, I was curling my arm around her waist and pulling her against me. Thought hadn't entered the equation.

She looked down, her eyes darkening. The soft thump when she set the wine bottle on the table should have nudged me out of this insanity. Yet, all I knew was I was tired, I was weary, I was tied up with need for her, and my emotions were a tornado inside. The only relief I could find would be with her.

Chapter Eighteen

AUDREY

Dallas curled his arm around my hip, pulling me close to him. My belly fluttered, and my pulse lunged as a wave of need rocked me. I could feel the slick heat between my thighs. I'd been wet ever since he flashed his crooked grin in the kitchen a few minutes ago. The effect he had on me was beyond ridiculous. I didn't care to really think about it anymore. Everything was raw, my emotions simmering right under the surface. I couldn't tamp them down, and they were all tangled up in my need for him. Intellectually, I knew I needed to get a handle on this, but right now I didn't care.

I stared into his deep blue eyes. All I knew was the need driving me.

"Audrey," he said gruffly, the sound of his voice alone sending a hot shiver over my skin.

Next thing I knew, I was straddling him. I could feel his hard cock rubbing against me. The friction of his denim jeans against my thin cotton leggings was sublime. I ran a hand through his hair, dragging my fingertips down along his jaw, savoring the rough scrape of his stubble. His eyes were dark, his breath coming in sharp bursts. My heart was pounding so hard, it almost hurt.

"Audrey," he repeated in a murmur, threading a hand into my hair and pulling me down to his mouth.

Kissing him was like a drug I couldn't get enough of. He took control, devouring my mouth with deep sweeps of his tongue, tugging on my bottom lip, his teeth sinking in. He was rough and wild, notching the need inside of me higher and higher. His hand tangled in my hair so tightly, I felt the sting of it in my scalp and savored the bite of pain.

He tore his mouth free, muttering my name, murmuring hot, dirty words as he kissed his way down my neck. The scrape of his teeth, the friction of his stubble on my neck sent hot shivers through me. He tore at my shirt, swearing when it caught on my hair.

He flung it aside and nearly ripped my bra off, cupping both of my breasts in his hands with a rough growl. My nipples were so tight they ached. He laved one with his tongue, drawing it into his mouth, sinking his teeth down to score it lightly.

I lost all sense of time as he set to drive me mad, teasing and toying with my nipples. I was rocking against him, spikes of pleasure scoring through me where his cock rubbed against my clit.

"Fuck, Audrey. You make me crazy," he muttered.

He lifted me swiftly off of his lap. I cried out. I didn't want any distance between us, but he was efficient. Within seconds, he had my leggings off. He slid his finger between my thighs, dragging it across the wet silk.

"You're wet for me, aren't you?" he asked in a gruff whisper.

Wordlessly, I nodded, crying out when he pressed against my clit with his thumb.

I reached between us, tearing his jeans open and shoving them down. His cock sprang free and then I was straddling him, forgetting I still had my panties on. He pushed them out of the way roughly. I sank onto him at once, crying out at the feel of him filling me to the hilt. I was restless and reckless, frantic to race toward my release. He gripped my hips and held me still, murmuring my name.

I dragged my eyes open to find his gaze waiting. The heated look in his eyes alone almost made me come.

"Slow down," he said.

I shook my head and rocked my hips against him.

His mouth hitched at the corner. "We can't go slow?"

I answered with another restless roll of my hips. I loved that he let go and let me take over. He released his grip on my hips, one palm sliding down my back while he toyed with my nipples with the other. He let me set the rhythm as I rode him. I rose up and sank down again and again and again. I couldn't get enough of the delicious stretch of him inside. I was on the edge for too long, pressure coiling tighter and tighter inside. I swore, and he reached between us. With a swirl of his thumb across my clit, I flew apart, pleasure raying through me. My channel clamped around him. He gripped my hips tightly, only now taking control, and held me down. I felt the heat of his release inside of me as he went taut, my name a rough cry.

My head fell into the dip of his shoulder as I tried to catch my breath. I felt wild and out-of-control, the only thing anchoring me the feel of his pulse pounding as hard and fast as mine.

DALLAS

I held Audrey against me, savoring the feel of her lush, warm body. I could've stayed there forever. We both lost control this time, and I didn't give a damn. After a few minutes, the timer went off in the kitchen, and she lifted her head. Her lips were swollen and puffy, her eyes still dark, and her hair a tumbled mess. Damn. She was the most beautiful woman I'd ever seen.

"I have to check on the lasagna," she said softly.

"So you do."

She slowly lifted herself, and I instantly missed being buried deep inside of her.

Not much later, we were sitting at the table, the fire flickering while we ate dinner. I considered what Russ had said today, that perhaps I could make room in my life for more than work. The crux was there was only one right woman, and I'd known that for years. She sat across from me just now. I simply had to figure out if I could bridge the chasm between the limits I'd set for myself and what I wanted.

———

The following morning, I woke before Audrey and reluctantly rolled away from her. Climbing out of bed, I had an almost visceral reaction to how much I wanted to stay there with her curled up warm and soft against me. I took a quick shower, forcing myself to go downstairs and get to work. Work would help me straighten out my head, or so I thought. With a fresh cup of coffee, I dug into the wall of emails updating me on the investigation since my interview the other night. My team had made another arrest in Connecticut. This was how investigations often played out. It was like dominoes. We'd catch a break and more would follow.

I was restless and antsy. Work usually kept me focused, yet I remained distracted. Audrey and my feelings for her were sending me in loops in my mind. Not long after I was up, I heard the shower running upstairs. The moment I heard her footsteps on the stairs, my body was on alert in anticipation. She came around the corner of the stairs into the archway and looked across the room. Her dark hair was damp, her cheeks rosy from her shower.

"Good morning," she said.

Molly's claws clicked on the hardwood floor when she trotted across the room, rubbing her head against my leg as I petted her. She wiggled madly, her tail thumping against the chair.

"Morning Molly," I said, flashing a grin toward Audrey. "Nothing like a morning greeting from a dog."

She laughed softly. "I smell coffee. Is there enough for me?" she asked.

"Of course."

She turned away, passing into the kitchen and calling Molly's name. Whether or not Molly actually knew it was her name, she understood the tone and immediately walked into the kitchen. I heard Audrey getting food for her. I tried to keep my attention on the screen, but my body was already on alert just having Audrey nearby. She returned to the dining room, sliding into the chair across from me where she'd set up her own computer. I glanced over.

"What's the status with your job anyway?" I asked.

"Well, I had the month off either way, so I figured I'd deal with it when I get back. Like you, I'm checking email here and there."

I'd never had a chance to talk with her about her legal career. I knew the basic details in passing from Thea, but I'd never inquired further. Not because I wasn't curious, but because feeding my curiosity about Audrey had been off limits for me.

"All I know from Thea is you're an Assistant Attorney General in the New York City office. Which division?" I asked.

She took a sip of coffee, swiping her tongue across her bottom lip and promptly distracting me. "I'm assigned to the Environmental Protection Bureau. I stay busy cracking the whip at businesses cutting corners," she said with a quick grin.

"I bet you're damn good at it. You never were one to back down from a fight."

Her smile widened. "I'll take that as a compliment. It's funny. It's easy to think this work isn't as difficult as the more hard core criminal stuff, but white collar crimes are nasty, and they fight dirty. I don't mind. I like buckling down for a long paper fight," she said, lifting one shoulder in a light shrug.

"So you like it then?"

"I do. My job isn't quite as glamorous as the defense attorneys who can charge a fortune. But I prefer to try to make a difference. Most of my cases are definitely the little guy fighting the big guys," she explained.

I suddenly had a ton of questions, realizing the wall I'd put up around hearing anything about Audrey had left too many blank spaces. She took another sip of coffee, and all I could do was watch her full lips close over the edge of the mug, her tongue swiping across her lips again when she set her mug down. My cock stiffened, and I shifted in my chair.

"How about you? Do you like your work?" she asked.

"I love it. It's my life," I said quickly.

As soon as I spoke, I realized my words were pure habit. I did love my job. I was damn good at it, and that meant something. Yet, Russ' comments rustled in my mind.

Audrey was quiet for a beat and then nodded. "So you say. Thea worries you work too much."

"Perhaps I do," I managed with a shrug,

beating back the emotion tightening my chest.

Audrey's phone rang, breaking into the conversation.

I forced my attention back to my computer while she took a call from what sounded like something related to her various wedding cancellations. Molly curled up on the floor where the sun fell through the windows. I settled in to work, as did Audrey after she finished her call. The morning passed quietly. At some point, I heard Audrey's breath draw in sharply as I was returning from the kitchen with another coffee refill.

I glanced to her as I sat down. "Everything okay?"

She took a deep breath, letting it out slowly before glancing back to me. "It's Matthew. He wants to argue about some of the wedding charges. Not exactly a surprise. He's also emailing and saying he wants to talk again. He didn't feel like it was fair you were there the other night." She rolled her eyes. "He's such a jerk. I wish I'd paid attention sooner. It sucks that it took him screwing one of my bridesmaids to get through to me."

Aside from swearing up-and-down about what an asshole Matthew was, I didn't have much to offer, so I nodded. "Need more coffee?" I asked when she lifted her cup and set it down upon noticing it was empty.

"I can..."

The ringing of her phone interrupted her.

"You get that. I'll get the coffee," I said, standing quickly and snagging her mug.

When I returned to the dining room, she was on the phone arguing with Matthew.

"Matthew, don't..."

I didn't know what he said, but I could hear the muffle of his voice, loud enough it was clear he'd raised his voice. Inside of a millisecond, I was furious. I reached over and snagged the phone out of her hand.

"Dallas!" she hissed, her eyes flashing.

I shrugged. I didn't give a damn if she was pissed. I lifted the phone to my ear.

"Leave her alone," I said clearly.

I ended the call and blocked the number before handing the phone back to her.

"I thought you blocked the number," I said.

She nodded tightly. "I did. He's calling from a different number now. I can handle this, Dallas. Let me handle it," she said firmly.

I stared at her, thinking I didn't want to let her handle any of it alone. Realizing I didn't have a right to make that demand, I recalled all the times Thea told me I could be high-handed. Right now, I didn't care to be anything other than that. I told myself I would feel the same way even if I hadn't been buried deep inside of Audrey last night. Yet, that was a fucking lie, and I damn well knew it. I didn't answer her. I simply nodded and sat back down at my computer.

Chapter Twenty

AUDREY

I rounded the corner, heading into downtown Haven's Bay. Thea had put me in touch with Julie, an old friend from high school. Julie was ever practical and not prone to drama. I figured it might be nice to grab a bite to eat and relax. I also needed a break from Dallas. Or rather, a break from how confused I felt about him. He'd totally pissed me off this afternoon when he got all high-handed and took the phone from me. I needed to handle Matthew myself. Yet, I also sort of savored how much Dallas cared about it. I kept reminding myself I needed to stay clear-eyed about what was happening with us. It was just an interval in time where we were letting ourselves explore this crazy chemistry between us. It would burn out soon.

I scanned the familiar landscape as I approached downtown. Christmas trees were decorated in yards with lights everywhere. The holidays made me feel nostalgic. While I didn't miss Matthew per se, I missed the idea of what I'd thought I was going to have with him. I wanted to be settled down, to feel like I had a touchstone in my life. I'd made the mistake of letting Matthew's initial charm blind me to so many other factors that so clearly showed we weren't right for each other.

I kept telling myself it was okay to let this play out with Dallas because there was an end date on it. He would go back to Boston, and I would return to my life in New York. The way he was acting about Matthew made no sense. If all we could have was sex, I didn't see why he'd have such a strong reaction to Matthew.

I pulled into Emile's, pausing to spin in a circle once I stepped out of my car. Emile's was in the center of downtown Haven's Bay, across the street from the old town green. Haven's Bay was lovely with its stately old homes and tall oaks and maples dotting the downtown area. Lights were hung festively with red ribbons twined around the light poles.

We'd had a windy, snowy night, leaving more fresh snow on the ground. The skies had cleared this morning, and it was cold and crisp. My boots crunched on the snow as I walked across the parking lot and pushed through the door into Emile's. I hadn't been here in years.

I was hit with a wave of nostalgia as I looked around. It was exactly as I'd remembered. Emile's was housed in an old cape style home. The hardwood floors gleamed with light falling in through the tall windows. Wooden tables were scattered in the middle of the main room with a coffee bar on one side, a liquor bar on the other, and a deli counter and kitchen in the back. From the mornings into the afternoon, it was a coffee shop and deli, and then in the evening, it was a bar. Leave it to small-town Maine to have a coffee shop, deli, and bar all rolled up in one. I waved at Emile who flashed a grin and a wink and kept on chatting with a couple of the guys at the deli counter.

Julie waved me over from a table in the corner. She stood and wrapped me in a quick hug before sitting down. I slid into the chair across from her, pulling off my gloves and sliding out of my jacket.

"Wow, you look great," I said. "You look the same as you did in high school."

Julie laughed. "Trust me, if you saw me in a bathing suit you wouldn't say the same thing. Two kids do remarkable things to a body."

I shook my head. "Cut it out. You look great."

"So do you," she said with a grin.

Julie had honey blond hair, blue eyes, round cheeks and a wide smile. She'd always been a down-to-earth friendly person. It had made perfect sense for her and Russ to end up together. They both had easy-going personalities and were family oriented. I couldn't imagine Haven's Bay without them.

"So how are the kids?" I asked.

"They're awesome. Some days they make me tired, but I wouldn't trade my life for anything. Little Russ will be in first grade next year, and Anna just turned four. I'm relieved to be done with the terrible twos and threes," she said with a laugh.

A waitress came to take our order. Julie caught me up on all the happenings in Haven's Bay. Her husband Russ was a good friend of Dallas'. He ran his family's timber and commercial fishing businesses. Julie had taken off a few years after she had the kids, and she was now finishing up college after-the-fact. She'd gotten pregnant when she was a junior in college. It hadn't been planned, but they'd gone with it.

When it came to her asking about me, I paused for a second, wondering what to say. I knew from her friendly call that she'd heard the news about my engagement, but she'd promised not to pry. That itself made me feel like I could talk with her.

"All things considered, I'm okay. I wish I'd broken things off sooner. Mostly I'm embarrassed. It sucks to realize Alyssa was screwing around with Matthew behind my back, but I'd rather know now. Honestly, I was so busy with work, he was so busy with work, and everything was crazy planning the wedding, I wasn't paying attention. I thought it would get better when things slowed down. But..."

Julie nodded, her mouth twisting in a rueful smile. "Well it's better that it happened now rather than after you got married."

"Trust me, I know. I've thought about that a lot since it happened. It sucks, but I'm moving on. I don't have much choice. My pride took a hit, but I'll get over it."

Ever since I'd spoken with Matthew at dinner a few nights ago, I'd managed to forget the embarrassment and how small I'd felt after finding him with Alyssa. Somehow seeing him had brought everything into sharp focus.

"How long will you be up here?" she asked.

Our waitress swung by to serve our sandwiches. After we were settled in again, I met Julie's gaze. "Well, when everything blew up, my plan was to come up here and stay for the month. We were supposed to be in Italy on a skiing trip. I don't want to go back to New York right now because then I'll have to face all of our friends. It's not a big deal, just a headache. I'm sure my parents would like me to come down there for Christmas, but then it's facing all of them feeling bad about what happened. I'd rather just do what I planned and take a break up here before I pull my life back together. Only thing was I didn't know my dad had asked Dallas to stay for the month. So, I have company."

I felt my cheeks heating. The second Dallas passed through my thoughts, I recalled the feel of him buried deep inside of me as I came apart in his arms.

Julie took a bite of her sandwich and eyed

me thoughtfully. When she finished chewing, she took a sip of water. "You know what Russ thinks?" she asked.

"Uh, no. What does he think?" I asked with a laugh.

She smiled a little. "He thinks Dallas has a thing for you. I *know* you used to have a thing for him."

My cheeks were burning hot now. I could hardly contain the rampant curiosity about what Russ thought. Julie was one of my other close friends back when we were growing up. Thea and I might have been best friends, but I could never have confided in her about my mad crush on her older brother. Yet, I had confided in Julie. She never knew about that fateful afternoon when I tried to seduce him. But she definitely knew I had a thing for him. Plenty of girls did. He was crazy hot and sexy. Even more so now.

I rolled my eyes and shook my head. "Seriously you're gonna go there?"

She leaned forward, lowering her voice. "Why not?"

I leaned forward as well. "Because I just broke up with Matthew. We were together for two years. I can't turn around and start up with somebody else right away," I hissed.

Of course, I wasn't sharing the fact I already had. But Dallas and I were just burning off some chemistry. Nothing more, so I reasoned it didn't count.

Julie didn't miss a beat. "So what? You just caught Matthew screwing one of your friends. The best revenge is to turn around and shove it right back in his face. Plus, if I read between the lines accurately, you and Matthew probably haven't had sex in months, so don't go acting like it's some big betrayal," she said with sly grin.

I rolled my eyes, leaning back in my chair and taking a sip of water as I looked over at her. "So maybe I had a thing for Dallas back then. Who didn't? My God, he was older and he was so hot. Now he's *Mr. FBI agent I don't do relationships.*"

"How do you know that?" she countered.

My cheeks got even hotter. I shook my head again. "Julie, it's not a good idea."

"Why not? He's hot as hell. Russ thinks he needs to get his mind off of work anyway. How would a little fun hurt either one of you?"

I'd forgotten how persistent she was. I simply shook my head. "Fine. You've made your point. Can we move on now?"

Julie rolled her eyes and shrugged. "Okay, just one more thing. Dallas is a good guy. No matter what he says, he's got a heart of gold."

Thankfully, she dropped the topic after that. Later that evening, I returned to the house. I'd been out longer than I planned, and it had started snowing again. It was dark, and the roads were slick. I walked inside, knocking the snow off my boots and hanging my jacket on the hooks by the door. Molly spun around my legs. I knelt down to greet her before she raced back upstairs. I could hear her jumping from the floor onto the bed in my old bedroom. She'd clearly decided that was her favorite place to be.

Dallas stepped into the entryway. His features were tense, and he looked almost angry.

"Everything okay?" I asked.

He nodded tightly. "Would've been nice to get a call. The roads are bad out there," he commented.

What the fuck?

I didn't realize I actually spoke aloud. His eyes narrowed.

"What do you mean *what the fuck?*" he asked.

I kicked off my boots and spun back to him. "What is it with you and being all high-handed? I grew up here. I can deal with driving on icy roads. You took the phone from me when I was talking to Matthew this morning too. What was that about anyway? You're not in charge of my life."

I was pissed. My emotions were riding high. Between the emotional upheaval in my life and tumbling into this madness with him, I didn't know how to deal with Dallas acting like this.

"Why are you worrying about any of this? It's just coincidence that you're here. If you weren't, I'd be doing exactly what I would be doing and I'd be fine. Like I am," I said, my tone mulish. I didn't give a damn how I sounded. I was just annoyed.

His eyes narrowed. "Fine," he said spinning around and stalking back towards the kitchen.

Once I was angry, I didn't back down. Whether my anger was logical or not at the moment didn't matter. It drove my actions. I followed him into the kitchen, reaching for his arm.

"Fine? That's it? Fine," I nearly spit out.

He spun around, his blue gaze darkening. In a flash, the air around us heated. I felt hot all over, need coiling tight in my belly, and my sex clenching. We stared at each other, the moment taut.

"Yeah, that's it. Fine. It's nothing," he replied, his voice low and controlled.

Oh, that did it. I was pissed he wasn't pushing back.

"It's not nothing. You can't just be all bossy with me. Maybe it's better if I just leave. If you're going to insist on staying here when it's entirely unnecessary, no sense in me getting in the way."

I started to turn away. He caught my arm as I spun around, reeling me against him. We collided right against the counter. He threaded his hand in my hair and his mouth slammed to mine. In an instant, our kiss went wild. It was hot and angry. His hand slid down my spine, pulling me roughly against him. The hard, hot ridge of his arousal pressed against me, right at the apex of my thighs. I needed to expel my frustration and anger, to burn up in the flames between us.

I tore my lips free, reaching between us and tearing his jeans open. Curling my palm around his cock, I sighed at the hot, velvety feel of the skin.

"Fuck, Audrey," he muttered.

I shoved his jeans down around his hips and knelt in front of him, dragging my tongue along the underside of his cock. I closed my lips over him, drawing him deeply into my mouth and savoring the salty tang of pre-cum. He yanked me up inside of a second. Our clothes were torn off, thrown in a tangle on the floor and then he was spinning me around, lifting me onto the kitchen counter, and dragging his fingers roughly through my folds. I was soaked with need for him.

"I need to taste you," he murmured, his voice husky.

He buried his face between my legs, his mouth on me. I gripped his hair. I could hardly take it. He licked every inch of my pussy, his tongue passing over my clit, sending sharp bursts of pleasure through me. He fucked me slowly with his fingers, bringing me to the edge again and again until I ordered him to let me go. He laughed against me, the vibration itself sending me over the brink when he drew my clit into his mouth. I was still reverberating from the shockwaves of my climax when he stood, bringing his lips to mine, his kiss passing the taste of me onto my lips.

Dragging my hips to the edge of the counter, he positioned his cock at my entrance and sank in to the hilt. He held still, his eyes locked to mine. I felt caught in his gaze, caught in this web of intimacy that wove us tighter and tighter together. He lifted a hand and brushed my hair back away from my face. Goose bumps chased along my skin where his fingers brushed as his hand slid down my neck.

"You had me worried," he muttered gruffly.

My heart thudded hard against my ribs. "About what?" I whispered, swallowing against the emotion cresting inside.

He was quiet, his gaze intense and searching. "You make me crazy. I know you can take care of yourself, but I don't like you being out when the roads are like this."

I didn't even know how to respond. My heart clenched. I sensed it took a lot for him to say what he'd just said.

"I'm fine," I finally murmured.

He nodded tightly. After a beat, he drew back slowly and sank inside again. I curled my legs around his hips, arching into him, a soft moan escaping at the delicious stretch of him filling me.

I needed it rough, fast, and hard. He gave it to me. There was no holding back. He drove into me, his hips pounding, my shoulders banging against the cabinet behind me, and I didn't care. My next release was upon me swiftly, crashing over me in an intense wave. I felt him go taut and the heat of his release filled me. His head fell into the dip of my shoulder. We stood there in the kitchen, our breath heaving. After a few moments, he lifted his head, his eyes catching mine. The moment felt too intimate, so intense I wanted to look away, but I couldn't.

Chapter Twenty-One

DALLAS

Several days later, I was scrolling through emails on my computer when my phone rang. I glanced at the screen to see it was my little sister.

"Hey Thea, what's up?" I asked.

"Dallas! Noah and Ian are coming up for Christmas. Isn't that awesome?"

I grinned because when Thea was excited, it was infectious. "It's great. Can't believe you pinned 'em both down."

"Oh, I had to do some sweet talking, but they're on board. I'm also calling because I was thinking maybe I could come up tomorrow. Audrey and I could drive down to New York together and deal with getting everything out of her apartment."

I'd mentioned to Thea that Audrey seemed open to help with this. "Sounds like a plan. How about I drive with Audrey? That'll save you a trip. Have you talked to her about it?"

"Not this specifically, but she said she was hoping to get it done before Christmas. I suppose it makes more sense for you to drive down," she replied.

"You can fly up later," I explained.

Thea chattered on for a few more minutes about how excited she was that Noah and Ian would be in Haven's Bay for Christmas.

"Have you been to the house yet?" she finally asked.

"No, I haven't. It looks the same from the outside. It's not like I don't know what's there," I added, biting back my annoyance.

I had mixed feelings about our childhood home. I hated the way it had come to me—through our father's backhanded efforts to protect his money. He'd put most of his investments in my name before the investigation caught up to him. I'd sold off everything and managed to pay off everyone he'd hoodwinked. The house was all we had left, and I didn't even know if I wanted to keep it. Thus far, I'd been ignoring it. The only reason I held onto it was because the home reminded me of our mother. It was more her home than anyone's, her presence permeating every memory I held of it.

"Geez, Dallas. Why are you so weird about the house? It's yours," Thea said.

I shifted my shoulders uncomfortably. "It's not mine, it's ours. In fact, I'm going to deal with processing the deed and signing it over to all of us."

I could practically feel Thea rolling her eyes.

"Whatever. I think you should keep it. You're the only one of us who visits Haven's Bay. It's obvious you miss it," she explained.

I didn't want to dwell on this line of conversation, much less point out I'd visited quite a bit less in recent years. "Mind texting me the address? I don't even know where Audrey lived in New York. You think we should give Matthew a heads up?" I asked.

Thea sighed heavily. "I don't give a damn. It's their place. She can go in and out when she wants, but I suppose we might as well check. I'll call. I'd rather her not accidentally walk in on him with Alyssa again. God, that whole thing pisses me off! How is she anyway? She hasn't called much, which worries me."

My mind spun back to last night. Every single day I woke up now and told myself I wasn't going to fuck Audrey senseless again. Every single day, I completely failed. Last night, I had my face buried between her legs and then my cock buried deep inside of her, watching her fly apart twice. She was like a drug I'd never known I could get addicted to. I was stumbling inside emotionally when it came to her, and I didn't know what the hell to do about it. She was coming to mean far too much, far too quickly. The sensible side of me knew I needed to step back, but I couldn't. For the first time in my life, my intellect wasn't running the show.

I forced my attention back to Thea.

"I think she's okay. Honestly, I do," I offered.

"Yeah, she actually sounded okay when I talked to her. I gave Alyssa hell for what she did. She's lost most of her friends over this. Fine with me, she can hang with Matthew and his asshole friends," Thea said angrily.

I heard Audrey's footsteps on the stairs. "Audrey's coming down. You wanna talk with her?"

Audrey came into the dining room with Molly trotting behind her. Molly was either asleep on the bed upstairs, or following one of us around the house. She was turning out to be an incredibly sweet dog.

"It's Thea. You got a sec?" I called out as Audrey stepped into the dining room.

Audrey glanced my way, her eyes brightening. I handed her the phone, beating back the urge to slide my palm over the curve of her bottom. Her comfort clothes consisted of a fitted V-neck t-shirt, which only made me want to lick into the valley between her breasts, and these swingy cotton pants that perfectly outlined her lush bottom. In short, she tempted me constantly. She talked with Thea as she walked into the kitchen to get coffee. A few minutes later she returned, handing me my phone.

"I hear you've decided we're going down to New York to move my stuff tomorrow," she said, catching my eyes.

"Thea suggested it, but I figured it made more sense for us to meet her there. You said it was okay, right?" I asked.

"It is. I just find it amusing how easily you make plans for others," she said with a roll of her eyes.

I stared at her for a moment, considering that I didn't usually make plans for anybody unless it was my family. Yet, I wanted her to be able to fully close the book on Matthew. That meant getting her stuff out of his orbit.

The question is why do you care so much?

Shut up.

I'd been telling my skeptical mind to shut up a lot. That question was quite pertinent and one I didn't care to consider. I didn't make a habit—ever—of pushing myself into anyone's life like this. Yet, I couldn't shake the hold Audrey had on me.

I didn't say any of these thoughts aloud and shrugged. "It was Thea's idea."

True, insomuch as Thea had brought it up. It was my idea to be involved, and I didn't care to discuss why.

Chapter Twenty-Two

AUDREY

Dallas maneuvered through traffic easily. I looked out the window, watching the mad cluster of traffic outside of New York City. We were crossing the Tappan Zee Bridge and would be exiting off to head into downtown Manhattan soon. The energy of the city pulsed, even from simply being in traffic on the outskirts. Dallas seemed unfazed by the madness and drove with calm assertiveness. I didn't know what to think that he was coming with me to help me move out of the apartment I'd shared with Matthew. To be honest, I didn't know what to think of anything related to Dallas anymore. Things just kept happening. Well, to be specific, *sex* just kept happening. We didn't talk about it, but every night, we tumbled into bed together.

During the days, he was often on his phone, working on his computer, and even participating in online conference calls. I wasn't sure how he could call this time a vacation. I kept myself busy visiting a few old friends in Haven's Bay and going through things in the house. I'd made arrangements for Sherry to take care of Molly while we were gone. The drive to New York was fairly uneventful. Thea had called ahead and said she'd let Matthew know we were coming by. I couldn't seem to banish the anxiety over encountering him again. I didn't know if he'd be there, or not, but I figured he'd be spoiling for an argument if he was.

It was strange to be spending this much time with Dallas. I'd stuffed my old fantasies about him so far into the distant reaches of my mind, I'd forgotten how alluring he was. With his dark hair, those deep blue eyes, and a body to die for, I was falling deeper and deeper into my fantasies about him. They weren't quite like the fantasies I had when I was younger. Back then, my fantasies were silly and vague. Now I had something real to hang them on. Sex with him was incredible, so crazy good just thinking about it made me wet. I kept thinking it would get less amazing. No such luck. Just now, I shifted in my seat, a little sore from last night.

Not much later, I directed Dallas into the parking garage. I rarely drove when I lived in New York, but the apartment building had a garage. I hoped against hope that Matthew's car wouldn't be in his assigned parking spot, and he would've had enough sense to stay away. Of course not. I should've known better. I didn't know if Thea had mentioned Dallas would be with me. Anxiety coiled in my belly, followed by a flash of anger. I didn't want to deal with Matthew. Ever since Dallas had blocked the other number he'd called from, I'd had enough sense not to answer calls from any unknown numbers.

When we stood outside the doorway, I hesitated, considering whether I should knock. I looked to Dallas, and he shook his head. He was so perceptive sometimes it was disconcerting.

"Don't knock. It's your apartment until you move out. After today, you'd have to knock," he said with a roll of his eyes.

I slid the key into the lock and let myself in. By New York City standards, we had a large apartment. By most standards, we had a tiny apartment. Just a living room and a kitchen with a short hallway that led to a bedroom and bathroom.

Matthew came walking down the hall. His eyes widened slightly and then narrowed when he saw Dallas. Matthew's dark blonde hair was rumpled and his eyes were tired, as if he hadn't been sleeping well. I wondered if he was still keeping himself busy with Alyssa. For his sake, I hoped so. Not because I gave a damn about her, but he might as well get something out of screwing me over. The thought made me recoil slightly inside. I wasn't upset at losing Matthew, but I was bitter about the way things played out. Being betrayed by two people at once definitely sucked.

Matthew started to say something when there was a sharp knock on the door. "It's me, Thea!"

I turned to answer the door.

"What are you doing?" Matthew asked.

"I'm answering the door. What does it look like I'm doing?"

"This isn't your place anymore," Matthew countered, his tone sullen.

Dallas arched a brow, his eyes narrowing. "It's her place until her stuff is out of here," he said sharply.

Part of me savored Dallas' protectiveness.

Matthew's eyes narrowed and his cheeks reddened slightly. With a roll of his eyes, he said, "Whatever."

I opened the door, letting Thea in. She squealed when she saw Dallas. "Dallas! I'm so glad you're here."

She flung her arms around him, and Dallas pulled her close with a wry smile. Thea had the same almost black hair and blue eyes a shade lighter than his. I'd forgotten how alike they were. Her personality was such a contrast. She was bubbly to his somber strength. My heart squeezed, a wave of emotion rocking me. It was always good to see my best friend, yet this emotion stemmed from seeing Dallas with her. It was as if every facet of him sharpened for me—those qualities that could seem hidden because of his tendency to be reserved. His warmth, his humor, how much family mattered to him— Thea brought all of those things to the surface, making my heart nearly ache for how much I wanted him.

———

Hours later, I returned to Matthew's apartment one last time to do a last walk through. Dallas was getting boxes organized in the back of his SUV. Thea had just left with a small load she was dropping off at her storage space. Since I didn't have any furniture, it hadn't been too challenging today. I had no plan for where I would go, but I would have the next few weeks to figure that out. When I stepped back into the apartment, Matthew was on his phone. I did a quick check, confirming there was nothing left.

I paused for a moment in the bedroom, recalling the last time I'd been here. Shock had rocked me when I'd opened the door to see Alyssa straddling Matthew. I swallowed the bitter aftertaste that rose in my throat. No matter that their shared betrayal of me had ended what I never should have started, it hurt. It was so embarrassing and just awful. Yet, his betrayal had served as the flashpoint I needed to act on what I'd already known.

Matthew hadn't lifted a finger today. Not that I'd expected his help. He'd sat sullenly on the couch, flipping through channels on the television for the few hours I was packing with Dallas and Thea's help. No matter my mixed feelings about Dallas, I was relieved to have him here. I sensed Matthew might have tried to push the envelope more if it had been just Thea with me. I walked down the hallway, pausing by the door.

Matthew looked up. When he noticed no one was with me, he stood, walking straight up to me. "What the fuck is going on with you and Dallas?"

Anger flashed inside. I didn't want to talk with Matthew, much less discuss anything to do with Dallas. Maybe it was a rebound, maybe it was a lot of things, but it was none of Matthew's business. He'd forfeited that when he screwed around on me.

"You don't have any right to ask! Matthew, you've been fucking Alyssa for how long now? Why don't you just go ahead and come clean about it?" I asked, annoyed and irritated.

"Fuck you, Audrey. It didn't have to be a big deal. I fucked up. You're the one who's turning it into a big deal."

"Oh my God, Matthew. I can't believe you. You were fucking my friend! She was supposed to be one of my bridesmaids. No matter what you think, what you did was shitty. Honestly, I'm relieved. We should've broken up sooner. You know it, and I know it. That's why you were fucking her. I wish you'd just had the nerve to tell me you were ready to move on."

Matthew snorted something, and then I heard the door swing open. Inside of a second, Dallas was at my side, his eyes locked to Matthew. Matthew glared at him.

"What the fuck, Audrey? Is he your body-guard now?"

"Matthew, shut up."

Dallas was quiet, too quiet. He was coiled tight, energy coming off of him in waves.

"Just leave it alone, Matthew. Leave me alone," I said, shaking my head. I quickly pulled the apartment key out of my pocket and set it on the counter. "We can consider this goodbye, Matthew. No matter how pissed I am at the fact you screwed one of my friends, I think it's for the best."

Matthew muttered something and turned to Dallas. "So you're fucking her, aren't you?"

Before I could react, Dallas had Matthew by the collar and lifted him off the floor. "It doesn't matter if I am. You don't talk to her like that. You have no fucking right. You're an idiot, and it's your loss," Dallas said, his tone low and laced with danger.

If Matthew meant to say something, he didn't. Dallas was clearly furious. I knew it wouldn't be a fair fight if there were one. Dallas had an edge to him. That edge turned me on and always had. It was subtle, but there was a depth to Dallas that few men shared. Matthew was nothing compared to him. He was all surface and gloss. Matthew muttered something and then Dallas flung him away, turning and grabbing my hand.

"We're going," he said firmly.

In another time and place, I might've been annoyed, but not now. I wanted to get the hell out of there. Within minutes, we stepped off the elevator into the parking garage. When we reached the car, I stopped and stared at Dallas. My emotions were a storm inside. Reeling from the reverberation of seeing Matthew, his betrayal fresh in my mind, the way I savored Dallas' protectiveness of me, how deep my feelings for him ran inside, and the confusion over what to do about any of it had pushed me to my limits inside.

"What am I to you?" I asked abruptly, the question tumbling out.

Dallas had been about to reach for the passenger door and let me in because he was that kind of guy. He spun back to look at me, his eyes narrowing.

"What do you mean?"

"Just that. We haven't seen each other in years. You act like nothing's been happening, but what is this to you? You said we couldn't have anything other than sex. Yet, here you are, helping me move and basically making sure I end things with Matthew. I don't get any of this. Why do you even care?"

For a millisecond, something flashed in his eyes, but he shuttered it quickly.

I didn't know why I was pushing, but I was unsettled and on edge. My voice was raised, echoing in the parking garage. Dallas simply stared at me. His hand dropped from the door handle, and he turned to face me, leaning a hand against the top of his SUV.

"Audrey, maybe we haven't seen each other in years, but you're Thea's best friend. Obviously, if you needed help, I would help. I wasn't trying to force you to move away from Matthew. I thought that's what you wanted," he said, his tone measured.

I hated that he sounded so reasonable. I also hated that he didn't even bother to address my question. He kept to the surface. I didn't know what I was pushing for. Something about seeing Matthew had set this off inside of me. Matthew reminded me of all the signs I'd missed before with him. I'd ended up wasting a lot of time, and now here I was having crazy, hot sex with Dallas and wondering what I meant to him. I gave myself a shake.

"Never mind," I said abruptly. "Let's just go."

For a moment, I thought he was going to argue the point. Part of me wanted him to. I might've known then if I meant more than I thought. But he didn't. When the silence began to stretch, he shook his head.

"Fine. Let's go."

The ride home was quiet. Dallas took a few phone calls, all of which were cryptic. He was always careful to keep his responses circumscribed. I had enough sense to know he needed to keep his work private, but it reminded me how unavailable he was to me, or anyone. No matter how much I wanted him for myself, I felt sad that he'd walled himself into this life where work was all he allowed himself. He was a good man with a good heart.

Thea thought everything that went down with their father had affected Dallas more than the rest of them because of his role in it. It's not that he'd been responsible for his father going to jail, but he'd been the investigator who stumbled across his father's financial crimes. I'd been just as shocked as everyone. Their family and mine had been close. I spent many a summer night at their house. Their mother had been an amazing cook, and she used to make heart-shaped chocolate chip pancakes for all of us in the mornings. After she died and then their father ended up in jail, they scattered. I knew they stayed in touch, but it wasn't the same. They weren't the family I had known once upon a time.

I couldn't help but wonder how deeply it had changed Dallas. I would've guessed his work would've been important to him before. I knew how hard he'd worked to get to that level in his career, but I'd never have guessed he would be committed to being alone.

Hours later, he pulled into the driveway, the snow crunching under the tires as we rolled to a stop in front of the house. He quickly carried our bags inside. Sherry had agreed to drop Molly off this evening, so when we came in, she scurried over to us, greeting us with wiggles and kisses. I loved how quickly she'd gotten attached, but then that's why I loved dogs. Dallas set his bag on the floor and knelt down to greet her. My heart clenched. It felt silly, but it meant so much that he loved dogs the way I did. That should've been my deal breaker with Matthew. Perhaps it would've been had I been living anywhere other than New York City at the time. I hadn't had a life where I could have a dog, so I didn't think about it much.

When Dallas straightened, he caught my eyes. He looked weary, and my heart squeezed again.

"Do you want me to unload everything now?" he asked.

I knew if I said yes, he would. He was that kind of man. I wasn't going to ask it of him. Not now.

I shook my head. "No need tonight. I'll figure out the rest over the next few days. It's not like I have to hurry."

We kicked our boots off. I snagged his jacket to hang up when it slipped from his hands to the floor. He glanced to me.

"Something hot to drink?" he asked.

"That would be nice."

"What's your job, the drinks or the fire?" he returned with a small smile.

The moment felt suddenly intimate. This was the kind of thing a couple did after a long drive. I nudged my chin in the direction of the kitchen. "I'll take care of the hot drinks, you start the fire. Do you want coffee, hot cocoa, or hot cider with a kick?"

"Hot cider."

I nodded and headed for the kitchen. Hard cider was a favorite in New England. With apple orchards spread across the region, autumn was a lovely time. Locals picked fresh apples and made cider to last through the winter. You could purchase fresh local hard cider at most local grocery stores. I'd picked up some from a local brewing company the other day. I fetched it out of the pantry and heated it on the stove.

When I walked into the living room, I found Dallas seated on the couch with Molly asleep beside him, her head resting on his knee. He was leaning back with his eyes closed. For a moment, I wondered if he was asleep. He lifted his head when I reached the couch, his eyes opening and his dark blue gaze colliding with mine. He straightened and reached for the mug of cider. I sat down on the other side of Molly, resting my hand on her hip as I took a few sips. The fire was flickering in the fireplace, its flames just starting to warm the room.

I woke hours later, held against Dallas' chest as he carried me up the stairs.

"I fell asleep?" I asked in a mumble.

Dallas chuckled softly. "We both did. I woke up when Molly whined to be let out. She's already back upstairs on the bed."

It felt so good to be held by him. He carried me into the bedroom. I stumbled out of my clothes and crawled into bed. It never even occurred to me to wonder whether he would be sleeping with me. He curled up behind me, pulling the covers around us, his palm warm on my belly under the cool sheets. I drifted back into sleep, feeling cozy and protected in his embrace.

Chapter Twenty-Three

AUDREY

I heard a squeal as I pulled my hair back into a ponytail. Walking downstairs, I found Thea stepping back from Dallas. Molly was circling Thea quickly, wiggling all over. It had only been two weeks, and Molly was finally starting to look a little less skinny. Thea glanced up at me.

"Hey Audrey, I came for the weekend since I have an extra day off."

I stepped to her, and pulled her into a hug. "Good to see you."

Dallas leaned into the archway leading into the dining room, his eyes bouncing between us. He'd been working more ever since we'd gotten back from New York City. Things had been also more tense between us. Oh, we still couldn't keep our hands off each other, not once the sun went down. Yet, during the day, he couldn't seem to put enough distance between us, staying busy with work almost constantly.

I'd been contemplating whether it might be best if I left and went to see my parents for the holidays. I had enough sense to call my boss the other day and extend my time off for another two weeks. Word had spread that my engagement was off. Fortunately, I had an understanding boss, and he'd easily agreed to the additional time off.

With Thea here, I knew the question about my holiday plans would come up. She was already expecting me to be here and had mentioned as much in a call the other day. She spun to Dallas, flinging her arms around him.

"It's so good to see you! That's twice in one month," she exclaimed. When she stepped back, she cocked her head to the side. "Why don't you look more relaxed?"

He arched his brow. "What do you mean?"

"You've been on vacation for two weeks." She looked to me. "He's pretty much working all the time anyway, isn't he?"

I caught Dallas' eyes and shrugged before

glancing back to Thea. "Pretty much. I suppose it's a little better because he's not working at the office until midnight like you say he usually does."

Dallas glanced between us and rolled his eyes. "Great, now I've got two of you." He chuckled. "How about I promise not to work for the weekend while you're here?" he asked, looking to Thea.

"I'll take it. What are we gonna do today?" she asked.

Dallas immediately glanced to his computer on the dining room table. "I need to finish up a few things and make some calls."

Thea sighed dramatically. "Fine." She looked to me. "What's your schedule for the day?"

"I don't have a schedule. You wanna grab a bite to eat in town?"

At her nod, I said, "Let me change, and then we'll go."

I jogged back upstairs, Molly shadowing me on the way up. I quickly changed out of my T-shirt and sweatpants into a pair of fitted jeans and a warm, fuzzy sweater.

In short order, Thea and I were driving down the coastal road into Haven's Bay. Just before we passed her family's old home, she slowed, glancing to me. "Do you know if Dallas has been by here?"

"I don't think so."

She turned into the driveway. "Let's go take a look. I asked him the other day if he was worried anybody would break in here. He didn't think so because the old alarm system is still on. I just don't get why he won't even stop by," she commented.

I didn't know what to say because I didn't have any answers. I looked ahead as we rolled down the winding driveway. Growing up with Thea, she and I had spent many an afternoon or night at each other's houses. Their home felt like a second home to me. It was a lovely house, sitting on the edge of a bluff that meandered down to a lawn with the ocean beyond. It was an old colonial home with two stories and white clapboard siding. Beautiful and stately, it had a widow's walk on the roof, an enclosed cupola with a clear view of the ocean, built for wives of sailors to watch for ships to return to shore. Thea and I used to love sleeping outside up there in the summer.

Dallas must've been hiring someone to plow because the long driveway was plowed and the front steps were shoveled. We rolled to a stop in front of the house. Thea glanced to me.

"This feels weird. The last time I came here, my dad wasn't in jail yet." She shook her head softly. "What a mess."

It was a mess, and I wished I could make it better for her, for Dallas, for all of them. Yet, I certainly couldn't undo what their father had done.

I wasn't sure if Thea wanted to go inside or not, but when she unbuckled her seatbelt and climbed out, I followed her. We stepped inside, knocking the snow off of our boots as we crossed the threshold. The house was quiet and held a feeling of emptiness, of a place where no one had been for a while. It was the same except all the warm touches were gone. There was nothing left here but furniture with sheets draped over it.

We walked through the foyer with the large curving staircase that led upstairs. To one side of the main entrance was a lovely, high ceilinged living room, what would've once been called the parlor. To the other side was a smaller room that led to a large kitchen and dining room. In the back was a screened porch that ran the full width of the house. The snow-covered lawn behind the house was quiet and untouched.

I followed Thea as she walked through the home. This was where she, Dallas and their two brothers had grown-up. When I was younger, a small part of me had once envied their family. They had been a wealthy family, yet their mother was loving and fun. While their father might've been distant, their mother set the tone for the family. I knew a bit from Thea about when things went sideways for their father. They didn't feel so lucky anymore because they lost everything but this house. We meandered through the upstairs, our footsteps echoing on the hardwood floors.

"God, this is depressing," Thea said softly when we were back at the main door. "No wonder Dallas doesn't want to come here."

She was quiet after we left. We didn't even talk about where we were going. We went to Emile's by unspoken agreement. We snagged the table in the corner. Emile wasn't here today. I didn't recognize the woman working the deli, or the waitress who came to take our order. Thea looked pensive. After the waitress brought us our coffees, I glanced over at her.

"Are you okay?"

She flipped her fork back-and-forth between her fingers and shrugged. "I guess so. That was weird. I've been nagging Dallas about the house, saying that we should do something. Now I kinda see why he's just sitting on it. It's the only thing we have left after all of it. It's sad to be there. It feels so empty."

"Do you think you'll ever come back here?" I asked.

"I dunno. I mean maybe we could rent it or something. It's just us now and none of us are in the same place."

"There's no rush. I suppose you'll figure it out. Were you planning to stay there for Christmas?"

Thea sighed heavily. "I thought we would, but it feels weird. Not to impose, but maybe we could stay at your place."

For a flash, I considered that would mean my nights with Dallas would have to be put on hold. I didn't dare sleep with him with Thea and their brothers around. It didn't mean I didn't want to. I shook my thoughts off of him. I considered the sleeping arrangement. There were four bedrooms upstairs, which meant somebody would have to bunk together.

"You and I could share a bedroom like old times," she said with a little laugh.

"You're welcome to stay. I'm still not sure if I'll be here through Christmas."

Thea's eyes narrowed. "Why? You said before you would be."

"I know, but my parents would love for me to come down there. I'm not sure," I hedged.

Our waitress arrived with our sandwiches. Conversation moved on. Somewhere along the way, Emile came in and stopped by our table, giving Thea a quick hug.

"Good to see you girls here," he said.

His salt and pepper hair was more salt now. His presence was steady and comforting, perhaps because we'd spent so much time here when we were younger. He and Thea chatted, catching up on all the Haven's Bay news. Not much later, we left. As we were turning into the driveway at my family's home, she glanced my way.

"How is Dallas really? I was so happy when he said he was coming here to check on the house. I thought it would give him a break. But it's like he can't even stop working," she said with a sigh.

More and more, I was coming to see his work was how he escaped from the rest of life. It tugged at my heart, yet I didn't know that he would let us be more than we were. I needed to remember that.

"I know. I suppose here at least he's not working late, so it's some kind of break."

Thea sighed. "I suppose. I wish he'd find something other than work to be passionate about."

My mind flashed to the way his hands and mouth felt when they were mapping my body, to the dark need reflected in his eyes when he was buried inside of me. I didn't quite think that's what Thea meant, but I knew there was one way he could let go.

Chapter Twenty-Four

DALLAS

"No seriously," Thea said with a laugh. "The guy was ridiculous enough to go into court and tell the judge the reason he was late was because his girlfriend threw a pizza at him. I swear, every time I think I've heard it all, I hear something else."

I chuckled and took a sip of wine, idly spinning the glass stem between my fingers when I set it back on the table.

Thea and Audrey had gone to law school together. Thea was a prosecutor in New York City and often shared funny court stories. I glanced between her and Audrey. Between the three of us, we'd almost finished a bottle of wine.

I hadn't had a night like this in years. Between my family splintering apart after my father was arrested and my careful efforts to limit contact with Audrey, I'd shied away from evenings like this. I was relieved for the table between us because it was near impossible to look at her without my cock stiffening. When she was relaxed, she was so beautiful she took my breath away. With her glossy dark hair falling loosely around her shoulders and her flushed cheeks, I wanted to drag her across table into my lap. But Thea was here. Unbeknownst to her, she was an accidental chaperone. For the entire weekend. I was going to need to keep my hands to myself. I couldn't have known how difficult that would be. I viscerally burned with need for Audrey.

Not much later, Audrey declared she was going to bed. I watched her walk upstairs with Molly shadowing her. I couldn't help it, but my ears paid attention to what room she went into. I knew she went into her bedroom, not the guestroom where we'd been sleeping. I heard the door close and gave myself a quick little lecture. I could sleep just fine across the hallway from her. It would be a good exercise in restraint.

Thea glanced over at me. "What's going on with you and Audrey?" she asked bluntly.

I stared at her, narrowing my eyes, trying to assess just what she might have picked up on. Thea was no idiot, and she knew me quite well. Just as she knew Audrey quite well.

I shrugged. "What are you talking about?"

Thea rolled her eyes and angled her head to the side. "You can hardly stop staring at her. Meanwhile, she's trying a little too hard not to look at you. I'm not an idiot. In fact, I'd be willing to bet something's going on with you two. It might be none of my business who you screw, but it's my business if it's Audrey. Don't fuck with her."

I wasn't ready for this conversation and was even less interested in dealing with my little sister lecturing me. I also felt a twinge of guilt because I was in so deep with Audrey, I couldn't see, much less think, past it.

"Thea, nothing's going on," I said firmly, lying through my teeth.

She leaned her elbows on the table and stared at me. "I don't believe you. I'm not gonna make you talk to me about it, but don't you dare mess with Audrey. She deserves a good man. I absolutely know you *are* a good man with a heart of gold. Your work is your life though, and you've made it very clear nothing else can get in the way of it. Audrey can't just be some fling you have."

Irritated, I drummed my fingertips on the table before quickly draining the last of the wine in my glass. "You know, Audrey's an adult. I think she can take care of herself."

"Well, now I know something's going on," Thea retorted.

"Whatever, Thea. Think whatever you want. I know she's your friend. I understand you want to protect her, but she can take care of herself."

More twinges of guilt stabbed at me, but I didn't want to entertain them now.

"I'm also not an asshole," I added, promptly wondering why the hell I'd said anything else.

Thea huffed. "I know you're not an asshole, but you don't make room for anything other than work. I'm all for you changing that, but don't you dare hurt Audrey."

"If you're so sure something's happening between us, why haven't you asked Audrey?" I asked, if only to be contrary.

Thea shook her head and rolled her eyes again. "If she wants to talk to me, she will. I'm not worried about you. I'm worried about her. As your sister, I'm asking you to respect her. She's already been hurt enough."

I knew I was feeling defensive and ready to argue with her about it. I forced myself not to. "Fair enough. You have my word I won't do anything to hurt her."

I went to bed that night, frustrated and hard. I ended up taking a shower in the middle of the night. I had to make do with taking care of myself since I couldn't get my thoughts off of Audrey. I recalled the feel of her channel clenching around me as I spurted my release against the tile floor in the shower.

I woke the next morning still irritated and feeling like an ass. I made the abrupt decision I'd return to Boston. It was the best choice. With Thea here, I was doing my damnedest to get a handle on my need for Audrey. I was quickly discovering the very act of trying to get my feelings under control only amplified them. I was nearly burning up inside for her.

Maybe putting a little distance between Audrey and me would help. I didn't like admitting it, but I needed an escape. Badly.

Chapter Twenty-Five

AUDREY

I stood in the kitchen, hands on my hips, staring at Dallas. "What?"

He stared back at me, his gaze inscrutable. "I'm leaving for Boston," he repeated.

"Oh," I finally said, scrambling my thoughts together. Inside, I was reeling—angry, frustrated and hurt. I didn't want him to leave. It hurt. I knew I'd been tiptoeing through dangerous territory with him, and now I knew why I should've backed away much sooner. "Does Thea know you're leaving?"

He nodded. "Yeah, I talked to her a few minutes ago. I spoke to Howard this morning. They arrested three guys on those burglaries, so you don't need to worry about that. Caught them in the act at a house on the other coastal road. They fessed up on breaking in here as well. I figure you and Thea might enjoy having a weekend together. I'll get back to the office and then return for Christmas. I'll probably stay at our house over Christmas."

His tone was flat and controlled. It annoyed the hell out of me that he was so matter-of-fact.

This is fine. You knew there was an end date. It's just coming a little sooner than you expected.

My heart cried out, stomping its feet and essentially pitching a little tantrum and banging around inside my chest. My stomach churned. I didn't want Dallas to see the turmoil I felt inside, so I turned away quickly and needlessly started washing a few dishes in the sink.

"When are you leaving?" I asked.

Thea was upstairs in the shower. Dallas and I had coffee together like we usually did in the short time we'd been staying here together. Thea, as usual, slept in quite late. She was most definitely not a morning person. I'd been in the shower when she must've gotten up.

"I already said goodbye," he said. "I'm just gonna run upstairs and grab my bag."

I took a steadying breath, rinsing the plate in my hands and setting it carefully in the dish rack before I turned around. I hoped I'd schooled my expression into a calm one.

"Okay," I said.

My vocabulary was failing me right now. There were so many things I wanted to say, but I couldn't think of how to say any of them. I shouldn't feel uncomfortable. This shouldn't be a big deal, yet I was so disappointed.

You knew this was going to happen.

Yeah, but I thought we had two more weeks.

Well, now you don't. This is why you never should've let this happen.

I shook my thoughts away and swallowed against the knot in my throat.

"Well, I suppose you should get going," I finally said.

Molly had been sitting in the middle of the kitchen floor. She stood and came over to me, wagging her tail and sidling up against my leg. I reached down to stroke her head. She might've only been with us for a short time, but I sensed she already knew me well enough to know when I was upset. I only hoped her canine powers of observation were much stronger than Dallas' human powers. He was more perceptive than the average person, but for once, I hoped like hell he couldn't see right through me.

He had that calm, distant expression on his face. He nodded tightly and turned away. I listened to his footsteps as he walked upstairs. I abruptly decided I would go for a drive. I didn't need to hang around to say goodbye. There was no sense in me hoping this was more than it had been.

I stuffed my feet in my boots, grabbed my jacket and keys, and called for Molly to come with me. Jogging outside, I let her in the car and started it quickly. As I rounded the circle at the end of the driveway and looked in the rearview mirror, I saw Dallas stepping out the front door. I was just close enough to see the look of surprise on his face.

Fuck him. Maybe I'd been stupid enough to agree to the limits he'd set, but it didn't feel any better to mean so little to him. I drove away quickly, concerned he might try to follow. Once I was on the coastal road leading to town, I turned off on another side road that led to a hiking trail. I pulled into the little parking lot at the end, put my car in park and just sat there.

My heart hurt. I felt so stupid. I'd fallen for Dallas a long time ago. I'd stuffed the feelings so far away, they'd been invisible to me, and I'd forgotten how he affected me. Molly nudged my shoulder. I stroked her head and buried my face in her fur, finally letting myself cry. I wasn't sure what I was crying for. I didn't know if it was Dallas, or all the time that I'd wasted with Matthew. I felt tired and alone, and I'd been so stupid to let myself get close to Dallas.

I couldn't convince my heart not to care. I leaned my head back against the seat after a few minutes and tried to gather myself together. I felt my phone vibrate in my pocket and tugged it out. Dallas' name flashed on the screen. I tapped the decline button and put my phone away. It was best if he left. I didn't need to read anything more into this than I already had.

I waited a little bit, only to hear my phone buzz again. I lifted it to see a text from him.

No goodbye?

"Dallas, there is no goodbye. We'll go back to the way things were for the last five years," I said to no one other than Molly.

She cocked her head to the side as if

trying to understand what I was saying, her brown eyes soft and curious.

"Human stuff. I was silly. I should've known better," I offered to her in explanation.

I stroked Molly's head, passing my hand down along her back. The bony ridges of her body were still easily palpable, but she was starting to gain some weight.

"Where should we go?" I asked, looking at her.

Molly had no answer, but she nudged my shoulder gently. I pulled out of the parking area and headed for a beach nearby where I used to walk the last dog I had growing up. It was usually deserted in the winter, and today was no exception. We walked along the sand, watching the waves roll to the shore and crash against the rocks up ahead. I savored the salty, icy air. Molly ran around like a maniac. She was good about coming when I called, so I let her run ahead and then spin back to meet me. She was like a little canine boomerang.

Even though my heart still ached, I figured it was time to go back and face Thea. I worried she would sense I was out of sorts. Well, out of sorts didn't quite capture it. I felt like I'd had my heart stomped on, and it was all the worse for the fact I'd put myself in this situation to begin with. I could blame it on Matthew. She didn't need to know I'd been silly enough to fall for her brother.

Chapter Twenty-Six

DALLAS

"What the hell?" I asked no one, tossing a file folder across my desk.

Cole poked his head around the door to my office. "Talking to yourself again?" he asked with a grin.

I rolled my eyes. "The team working on that money laundering investigation came up with a whole lot of nothing. It's been two weeks, and I was hoping they'd make some headway while I was gone."

"Dude, you do *not* know how to take a vacation."

"What do you mean?" I countered.

He stepped into my office, slipping into the chair across from my desk. "You've been gone two weeks, and all you can do is bitch about what nobody did. You know some-times it takes months to catch a break on in-vestigations. Especially in finance cases. It's your specialty, you know this," he said with a slow shake of his head.

I leaned back in my chair, running a hand through my hair. "I know. No need for me to get pissed over nothing."

I stood abruptly and rounded my desk, stepping to the coffee pot in the corner. I quickly poured a cup, holding it up aloft. "Coffee?"

Cole shook his head. "I'm wired enough already, but thanks."

I returned to my chair, slouching into it and taking a sip of coffee.

"What is it?" Cole asked when the silence started to stretch.

I angled my head to the side. "What do you mean?"

"You," he said, lifting his hand as he ges-tured toward me before letting it fall. "You've been a jerk, to put it bluntly, ever since you've been back. You're cranky as hell and irritated about everything. This isn't like you. One of the reasons you've had a solid team all these years is because you're easy to work with. If you keep this up, it won't stay that way."

I stared at him. "That bad?" I asked.

Cole nodded vigorously. "Oh yeah, man. You're like the office cactus right now. No one wants to get too close."

I burst out laughing. "All right. Fair enough. Guess I gotta work on my attitude."

Cole shrugged. "You don't have to. If you want to cultivate a reputation as an asshole..."

"Not what I'm after," I said with a roll of my eyes.

"Wanna talk about what's going on?"

I held his gaze for a moment, suddenly recalling my conversation with Russ back in Haven's Bay. Cole was the very friend Russ had been referencing when he said one of my buddies from work had a family. I'd been Cole's best man at his wedding three years ago. He and his wife had a two-year old and a baby now. He'd found a way to juggle the needs of his family and his job and make it work. It's not as if I hadn't known this, yet I hadn't contemplated what it could mean for me. I'd so effectively shut off the idea of settling down because once I'd known Audrey was engaged, I'd told myself it was for the best. Everything had changed now.

"How's Shelly?" I asked abruptly.

Cole didn't miss a beat and accepted the change in topic. "She's good. Sara's sleeping through the night finally, so life is great." He laughed softly. "If you ever do settle down and have kids, trust me when I say you'll hardly sleep when they're babies. I was tired as hell all the time until they made it through the night. Your standard for a good night's sleep gets so low that if you make it for four hours, it's like 'oh sweet Jesus, that was heaven.' I think I had my first full night of sleep in a year and a half the other night. Those people who talk about how great it is that their baby sleeps through the night? They should be slapped," he said with a laugh.

I chuckled along with him and took a gulp of my coffee. "I could handle the sleepless nights. I've never been much of a sleeper as it is."

"Well, there's a mark in your favor. Tell me how come you're back from your vacation early."

I shrugged. "No need for me to stay. Thea's there now. They arrested the guys responsible for all the break ins. Audrey'll be there past the New Year anyway. Just no reason for me to stay."

Cole nodded slowly and picked up a pen from my desk, flipping it back and forth between his fingers. "Something up with you and Audrey?"

"No. Why do you ask?" I countered, instantly guarded.

"Because Thea mentioned it to me when she stopped by to pick up those files you wanted the other day. She thinks something might be going on. You know Thea. She's worried about Audrey and you at the same time."

Oh, did I ever know Thea. I rolled my eyes. "Look, it's no big deal. I might've stepped in it, but I can straighten it out."

Cole arched a brow. "What do you mean?"

I sighed and leaned back in my chair. "I might've let something happen."

Cole was quiet for a beat, his gaze considering. "By *something*, I assume you mean you screwed around with her."

"Look, I..." Fuck. I hated knowing Thea was nosing around, and I hated having Cole look at me like I was some ass. "Audrey knows there's no room in my life for anything other than something casual. It's probably best I came back early."

Cole held my gaze, shaking his head slowly. "Not if she's the reason you're such a fucking asshole," he said.

"Man, I'm just tired, okay? Give me a few days to get back into the swing of things."

"See, that's the thing. You're not supposed be tired after two weeks off, so either you were burning up the sheets and not getting any sleep, or you're not tired and you're just cranky because you might actually want more than a few nights in bed with her."

I wanted to swear and tell him to shut the fuck up, but that might just prove his point. I played it cool and shrugged it off. "Leave it alone. I'm fine."

"Fair enough," he finally said. "Work on your attitude in the meantime."

At that, he stood and left. I leaned my elbows on my desk and ran both hands through my hair before straightening. I took another gulp of coffee, my eyes landing on the clock above the door. It was going on seven o'clock at night. I was restless and antsy. It was fairly common for me to work until eight or nine at night, but I didn't even want to be here. I was too distracted and too frustrated. I missed Audrey. I hated that I hadn't gotten a chance to say goodbye. She'd taken that chance away from me and hadn't answered a single text or call since then. I wanted to ask her why the hell she wouldn't let me say goodbye. I wanted to ask her all kinds of things. But I didn't.

Give it a few weeks. You'll be back to your game.

I wanted to punch that voice because, right now, I was pretty damn sure a few weeks wouldn't make the ache in my heart go away.

Chapter Twenty-Seven

AUDREY

Thea stared at me, her eyes wide and her mouth open. She snapped it shut. "You had a crush on Dallas back in college?"

I felt my cheeks heat. With a sigh, I said, "Whatever. It was a long time ago."

"Obviously, not that long ago if you still have a thing for him now," she countered bluntly.

Julie glanced between us. "Who gives a damn if she had a thing for Dallas back in college?"

"I just can't believe you didn't tell me," Thea said with a glare.

"Oh my God! I didn't tell you because he's your older brother. Plus, he's ten years older than us. Back then, it seemed like a lot. Not so much now."

"Okay, so let me get this straight. You're moping around, not because you caught your ex-fiancé screwing Alyssa, but because you started screwing my brother. Apparently, Dallas was your forever crush or something, and you still have a thing for him. Do I have it right?" Thea asked.

I glared at her, annoyed with how direct she was. "Could you calm the hell down? You're making it into a huge thing."

Julie shook her head with a laugh. "I think she's in shock. Apparently, she didn't notice Dallas was totally hot back then and half of her friends had a thing for him."

"Oh, *I* didn't think he was hot, but I knew other girls thought he was. He's my brother and you're my best friend. Why didn't you just tell me?" Thea asked with a sigh.

Thea's long weekend had turned into five days. She'd taken the rest of the week off. She'd gotten pushy with me this morning at the house because she'd declared I was moping and depressed. Even though I hadn't wanted to admit it, she was right. I'd finally broken down and told her what happened with Dallas. We were having an early dinner at Bay Bistro with Julie. I was downright relieved to have Julie there because she was obviously calmer than Thea about the whole thing.

"Your reaction now is why I never said anything before. Plus, it's not like it was gonna go anywhere back then. It's not going anywhere now. I screwed up. I shouldn't have let anything happen, but I did. Now I'm all messed up over him. I feel weird because I should be upset about Matthew, and I'm not. I mean, it sucked to catch him screwing Alyssa, but that's about it. I just feel like an idiot for not catching onto him sooner."

Thea held her empty wine glass aloft when she saw Sherry threading through the tables. Sherry reached our table and glanced to Thea. "I suppose you'd like some more wine."

"Oh, I *need* more wine," Thea declared.

Sherry arched a brow in question.

"Audrey has a thing for Dallas," Thea announced with another aggrieved sigh.

Sherry put a hand on her hip and narrowed her eyes at Thea. "Tell me something I don't know, and what's that face for?"

"Because he's my brother, Thea said.

"So? They're both adults. They can do whatever they want. Let it go, girl," Sherry countered.

Thea leaned back in her chair. "I know. I'm just getting used to the idea, okay?"

Sherry chuckled and glanced between us. "How about you ladies? More wine?" she asked.

When Julie and I nodded, Sherry glanced at the clock on the wall above the bar. "That's it. I'm calling Russ. He's gonna have to be your designated driver."

Julie giggled. "Oh, he'll do it. I already warned him I might call for a ride. It'll be more fun if you call though."

Sherry rolled her eyes, sliding her phone out of her pocket as she walked away. Julie managed to steer Thea away from her obsession over being offended that I hadn't told her about my crush on Dallas five years ago. Little did she know how bad it had been. I was glossing over it and making it sound like nothing more than a little college drooling over a hot older guy. How did I tell my best friend that I'd fallen head over heels in love with her brother? Giving in to the desire between us had sent my heart spiraling. I'd intellectually known Dallas didn't want more than sex—hell, he'd made a point to say that was all we could have. Yet, my mind couldn't ease the folly of my heart.

Julie chatted about her kids and steered the conversation onto local gossip and the usual curiosity about who was where in life now. At some point, Thea left to go to the restroom.

Julie glanced at me. "You've got it bad for Dallas, huh?" she asked softly.

Tears pressed hot at the back of my eyes, and I swallowed against the tightness in my throat. "I guess so. I should've known better. It's just…"

I paused to gather myself, and she curled her hand over mine, giving it a squeeze.

"It's okay. We can't always control who we fall for. I'll remind you Russ is pretty damn sure Dallas has a thing for you. Russ thinks he has for years. I think you shouldn't give up."

"Oh? Well, what the hell should I do?" I asked, frantically trying to beat back the hope that wanted to dance in circles in my heart.

"Maybe tell him how you feel. I think you're gonna have to push Dallas on this. That's just how he is. That doesn't mean he doesn't care, it's just not how he expresses himself. You forget I know him too."

I stared at her, wrestling with hope, fighting my tears, and wishing my heart didn't ache so much. It had been four depressing days ever since Dallas left. I'd blocked his number from my phone when he tried to call me the first day after he left. I didn't need reminders of what I couldn't have.

Thea returned to the table and looked between us. "You look sad again."

The tears I'd been holding at bay spilled over.

"Oh God. You really like him," Thea said as she slipped into her chair and leaned her elbows on the table. "This isn't just a sex thing, is it?"

I shook my head, and grabbed a napkin off the table. I swiped at my tears and balled the napkin in my hand. "No, it's not just sex. I need to get a grip though."

Julie looked over at Thea. "I think she should tell Dallas how she feels. What do you think? You're his sister."

Thea was quiet for a beat. She appeared to have moved past her annoyance I hadn't told her about my crush. "Well, you and Dallas would be great together, actually," she said softly. "Dallas has a heart of gold, and he takes care of everybody. I think it killed him what happened with our dad. We lost pretty much everything except the house. He stepped in and cleaned up the mess for everyone. Hell, he took care of everybody our dad screwed over. Ever since that happened, he just buried himself in work. He was different before. It's like he just decided he wasn't gonna let anybody in after that. Julie's right though. I think you should tell him how you feel. If anyone could get through to him, maybe it would be you."

I stared at Thea and took a shaky breath, quickly blowing my nose. The idea of telling Dallas how I felt made me half-terrified because if he rejected me then, it would dwarf the hurt I'd felt so far because it would be final. Yet, the only way to get to the other side of my heartache was to face it head on. If there was a chance for us, this might be the only way to find out.

"All right, I don't know if I can, but I'll see if I can work up the nerve."

"Well, don't waste time. He's grumpy as hell right now. I talked to him last night, and he sounds, well, he just doesn't sound good. Now I have a better idea why," Thea said with a soft laugh. "Do you want me to talk to him? I already gave him a lecture on leaving you alone," she asked.

I shook my head. "No. I need to do this."

Sherry arrived with our fresh glasses of wine. Thea lifted hers in a toast.

"To you and Dallas. You can figure this one out. I just know it. You'll get your crush, and maybe he'll stop hiding in his job," she said, her eyes glittering.

Chapter Twenty-Eight

DALLAS

I glanced at the clock above my office door. It was close to midnight, perhaps a little later than usual, but not insane for me to be at work at this hour. I stood to pour another cup of coffee and returned to my desk. Spinning my phone around, I stared at it for a moment. Checking my phone had become an annoying habit over the last few days. For probably the thousandth time, I pulled up Audrey's name in my contacts. She hadn't responded to any of my messages or texts. I was beginning to wonder if she'd actually blocked my number. My fingers moved of their own accord. I quickly typed out a text. This one different from all the others I'd sent so far.

I miss you. I wish I'd had a chance to say good-bye. I don't suppose there's any chance we could talk?

My thumbs hovered over the screen as I considered what else to say. Coming up blank, I hit send and then set the phone down. Cole had been on me, pointing out yesterday that I was still a cranky asshole. His words, not mine, although I couldn't disagree. It had been a full week since I'd departed Haven's Bay. Christmas was a week away.

I'd have thought by now I would've gotten past the ache in my heart. I wasn't sleeping well. At all. I missed having Audrey beside me. It was incredible how quickly I'd gotten used to sleeping beside her. It wasn't just the sex I missed. If anything, I missed her simple presence the most. I'd been accustomed to sleeping alone all the time for years. In fact, when I did date, I went out of my way to avoid letting things get too intimate. Yet, inside the span of a few nights of sleeping with Audrey, I didn't like sleeping without her warm, lush body beside me. At all.

Working until midnight had become a habit this past week, if anything because I didn't want to go home to my quiet, empty apartment. I spun away and clicked onto my computer screen again, opening up a report from a team in our New York Office. They were handling one arm of a massive financial investigation. My vision was bleary, and I clicked away quickly because I was too tired to process any information. Instantly, I was staring at my phone again as if willing Audrey to reply.

Dude, it's midnight. She's probably asleep.

Logically, I knew that was probably the case, but I didn't want it to be. I wanted her to miss me as much as I missed her.

If that's what you wanted, maybe you shouldn't have left the way you did.

Oh, shut up.

Aside from my own internal arguments, I'd replayed my conversations with Russ, then Thea and then Cole repeatedly, trying to sort out what it all meant. There'd been a damn good reason I put up boundaries between Audrey and me years ago. I'd wanted her too much, and she was too young. She deserved somebody other than a man like me.

Yeah. Look how that worked out. She ended up with Matthew, the fucking asshole who screwed her friend.

I gave my head a shake, snagged my phone off my desk and my jacket off my chair, and left. I needed to attempt to get some sleep. I drove through the cold, still night down Boston's narrow streets to my townhouse in Charlestown. I lived in a nice part of Boston near the Charles River in a townhouse, and I hardly ever spent time here. I let myself in, dropped my keys on the table by the door, and flipped on the light, scanning the quiet space. Once upon a time, as recent as a month ago and before a few weeks of Audrey had made me lose my mind, I used to enjoy coming home to nothing more than peace and quiet. Every so often, I might grab dinner with a date who had no expectations. Aside from a few friends at work, that was the extent of my social life.

I fell asleep into a restless sleep. Sometime in the wee hours of the morning, I woke to the sound of my phone buzzing. I rolled over in the darkness, snagging it off the nightstand and expecting to see a call from somebody at the office. The clock on my phone read 4:00 AM. Audrey's name flashed on the screen.

I sat up abruptly, propping myself on the pillows against the headboard. Giving my head a shake to nudge me out of sleep, I swiped the text to open it.

I'm sorry you didn't have a chance to say goodbye either. We can talk if you'd like.

Even though it was just a text and there was no real way to know how she felt, her reply felt dry and controlled. There was that side of her and then the fiery, feisty side.

I wanted more, so much more. It was strangely gratifying to realize she was up at this hour texting me. I wished I were in Haven's Bay, so I could wake up beside her. For a moment, I considered what to say.

I didn't particularly care to keep pretending though, so I stopped trying to plan my response and simply typed what I felt.

I meant what I said. I miss you.

The little dots appeared, indicating she was replying. My heart twisted in my chest, and emotion lashed at me. This was an unfamiliar place for me. After a moment that felt like forever, her reply came through.

I miss you too.

What are you doing?

:-) Sitting in my bed, having trouble sleeping. What are you doing?

I chuckled to myself.

Same thing. I miss sleeping beside you.

After my last comment, I didn't see the dots appear, and I wondered if she was going to reply. After another minute or so, they appeared and my heart eased slightly.

I'm not sure what you're doing. You said we could only have sex. It was probably stupid of me, but I accepted that limit. You're confusing me now.

I stared at her text. Fuck. I leaned my head back and stared at the ceiling. She had every right to point that out. I had set some clear limits. Unless I knew what I wanted, I needed to be careful. I looked back down at the phone and decided maybe I should just be honest about how mixed up I was.

The only reason I pushed you away five years ago was because I thought you should have a chance to see what you wanted first. My life isn't simple. I respect the hell out of your father. He's the next closest thing I have to a father after everything that my dad did. I don't know if this is making any sense, but I was trying to respect him and you.

Another long pause with my heart in my throat and my gut churning while I waited for her reply. I wondered if she was going to ignore what I said. The little dots appeared and went on for a bit. I considered myself a patient man, but it was fucking hard to wait.

Oh. All this time I didn't understand how you felt back then. Would've been nice if you'd told me sooner. Thea told me I should tell you how I feel so here goes. Five years ago, I had a crazy crush on you, like the worst kind. I thought you thought I was ridiculous after what I did. I never stopped wanting you, but I set out to find somebody else because I thought that's what I needed to do. You saw how well that went. It's not just sex for me. It never was. I love you.

Chapter Twenty-Nine

DALLAS

I love you.

I felt as if I was suddenly falling from a great height, my stomach felt hollow and emotion churned like a storm inside of me. I stared at Audrey's text. I was alone in my apartment at a few minutes past four in the morning. My heart was pounding so hard and fast, you'd think I'd just run a race. I generally considered myself prepared. Yet, I wasn't prepared for this. My thumbs hovered over the screen as I contemplated how to respond. I'd had a vague idea that I would tell her I missed her, and she'd stop shutting me out. I hadn't thought beyond that. Perhaps I could go see her in New York on the weekends. My reaction against love wasn't about Audrey per se. It was about how I knew everything could blow up and scatter.

My mother had been the glue that held our family together. In hindsight, she was probably the only person who kept our father from being stupid sooner. Her stroke had sent all of us spinning sideways, and I still grieved her loss. My father, whom I had once admired despite his distant way of parenting, had disappointed me so painfully and betrayed so many people. Letting yourself love someone meant setting yourself up for loss. Audrey should know that after what Matthew did. Even though it sounded like she hadn't quite loved him, she'd given him her trust.

It wasn't that I didn't trust Audrey. I trusted her completely. It was just...

Fuck. I must've waited too long before replying. My phone vibrated in my hand again, and I looked back down at the screen.

Okay, I went too far there. I don't expect you to want what I want, or to feel the way I feel. I just needed to let you know how I felt. We can go back to the way things were and see each other once in a blue moon. I won't be a cliché.

What the hell did she mean?

Cliché?

Her response to my single word question was swift.

Hoping and waiting for something that's never going happen. I shouldn't compromise just for the sake of compromise. I'll wait and the right person will come along, but I won't be that cliché person who waits for someone only to wait alone forever. I'd say have a good night but morning is already here.

Even though I couldn't see Audrey, I could feel the sadness in her.

I won't be here for Christmas. I'm turning my phone off now.

Wait.

She never replied to my last request, and I never fell back asleep.

———

Several days later, I was back at the office when Cole came around the corner into my office. "Hey cranky," he said by way of greeting.

I glanced up and rolled my eyes. "What can I do for you?"

"The New York team helping on that messy finance case wants to have a conference call this morning. You got time?" he asked.

I glanced at the clock above the door behind him. "I've got another meeting in an hour, so now would be better. Can you make that work?" At his nod I continued, "Where? My office or yours?"

Cole glanced around my office and shrugged. "Can I start some coffee?"

At my nod, he stepped to the small table in the corner and started a fresh pot. He tapped the button and spun around to slide into the chair across from me.

"You look like hell," he said conversationally.

"You don't say?" I asked.

"I do," he replied with a chuckle. "You've looked like hell for a full week now. When are you due back in Haven's Bay?"

"Day after tomorrow."

I batted away my near constant thoughts of Audrey. I'd been seriously considering telling Thea I needed to cancel my part in her plans for Christmas, but I knew she'd be disappointed. This would be the first Christmas all of us had spent together since the year after my father went to jail.

Cole promptly zeroed on the very topic I

preferred not to discuss. "What's new with Audrey?"

"Nothing. Why do you ask?"

I managed to keep my tone level, but the second he mentioned Audrey's name, I was irritated. I didn't need anyone pushing me on this. I'd screwed up, and I just needed a little more time to return to my baseline.

Cole shrugged. "Oh, maybe the fact you've been more of an asshole for the last few days. Kinda made me wonder if something was up."

An angry weariness hit me. I missed Audrey like crazy, and I was pissed off about it. It had been radio silence from her. My last response to her, an entire single word asking her to wait, had been met with complete silence. The following morning I'd texted her again.

Can we try this again?

Still nothing.

At my silence, Cole angled his head to the side. "You know, you could ask for advice if you ever wanted it. I know that's not really your thing, but there are some areas where you're not the expert."

I shifted my shoulders and rolled my head in a circle, trying to ease the tension in my neck. I'd been beating back a headache for what felt like days at this point. Ibuprofen was doing nothing more than keeping the edge off of it.

"What the hell do you mean?" I finally asked.

"All I have to do is say Audrey's name, and you look at me like you're ready to punch me. You don't have much of a temper, so I figure it's a sore spot. What gives?"

Fuck it. I quickly summarized my last text conversation with Audrey.

After I finished, Cole stared at me, his mouth hanging slightly open. The coffee maker beeped.

"Hang on. I need coffee for this," he said. He stood and poured a cup, looking in my direction. "Want some?"

At my nod, he stepped to my desk and set the cup down quickly before returning to pour another cup for himself. Once he was seated, he took a long swallow and then met my eyes.

"Okay, let me get this straight. She told you she loved you and some other stuff, and you said 'wait.' Do I have that right?" he asked.

I sighed. "Yeah, that about sums it up."

"If I'm getting this right, you want to have some kind of something with her, but you're not sure what it is," Cole added. He leaned back with a sigh, shaking his head slowly. "Man, you're an idiot. Here's the thing, if she loves you and she wants more and you don't, then you need to leave her the hell alone. That's it. It's the only fair thing to do. Is that what you want?"

I fucking hated his questions. I took a gulp of coffee and eyed him. "Well, I know I want to see her."

"Yeah, but she loves you. So, if there's not even a chance of more than being fuck buddies, you can't see her. It's not cool."

Cole actually looked pissed off.

"Man, I'm not trying to be an asshole," I muttered.

"Oh I didn't say you were being an asshole. You *will* be an asshole if you try to take things further and you know you don't want more. That's all I'm saying."

Emotion rocked me. Fear mingled with longing. I was afraid to lose this chance with Audrey, and I was furious with myself over the whole mess. I did *not* enjoy feeling out of control of my emotions.

"You want my opinion?" he asked.

I stared back at him and finally shrugged. "Sure. What's your opinion?"

"I think you're stalling because you want

more, and you don't know what the hell to do about it. I've been married to Shelly for three years now, and we were together for three years before that. It's not always easy. I'm not saying that I ever wonder whether I love her because I don't. But life is messy. Some days I'm in a bad mood, and some days she is too. Throw two little kids in the mix, and it gets even more challenging. That's what commitment's about. You deal with whatever comes your way. The easy stuff is a piece of cake. Great sex, fun dinners, days when nobody's tired—those are the good days. It's sticking it out when it's not so easy that matters."

I stared at him, my gut churning. I finally nodded tightly. "Fair enough. Why do you think I want more?"

"Because if you didn't, you would've let her go already. I'm joking around about it because I can deal with it, but you are seriously being a jerk around the office. You're cranky, and you're on edge all the damn time. I'd say you just need a good lay, but I don't think that's gonna cut it."

I let out a sharp laugh, startled when it came out. "That bad, huh?"

"Well, I mentioned it a week ago. Hasn't gotten any better. I think you need to decide what you want to do. Either you let her go, and I mean *really* let her go, or you stop being so damn scared about facing this."

I took another gulp of coffee and nodded slowly. "I appreciate your opinion," I finally said.

Cole chuckled. "Anytime, man. Now let's make that call."

Chapter Thirty

AUDREY

I stacked a box in the corner of the garage and stepped back. Blowing my hair out of my eyes, I dragged my sleeve across my face. I'd spent the morning organizing the boxes we'd unloaded from Dallas' SUV before he left. I didn't have enough room to take them back in my car, and I didn't even know where I would be moving yet. For the short term, Thea had invited me to stay at her place until I found a new apartment.

Christmas was two days away, and I planned to leave tomorrow morning to go see my parents. Thea had tried to persuade me to stay in Haven's Bay, but I just wasn't up for it. This afternoon, she'd headed over to her family's old home. She was busy taking the sheets off the furniture with Julie and Sherry's help, trying to make the house feel like a home again. I didn't think I could deal with seeing Dallas, not right now.

The only good thing that came out of me being stupid enough to give in to my desire for him was perhaps this time I would be able to truly move on. Before, I just hung onto my crush. I might've buried my feelings, but they'd always been bubbling under the surface. This time, I wouldn't compromise. I would let go. In the far reaches of my mind, I would no longer wonder whether there might be a chance for us. Dallas had made it perfectly clear there wasn't.

I walked to the last box, lifting it and stacking it on top of the last row. My life was in boxes now. These boxes would wait here for me until I had time to come back. I wiped my dusty hands on my jeans, turned off the lights and walked outside, locking the door behind me. Molly came dashing to me from the yard, snow flying around her as she bounded through it. I grinned and managed one stroke on her back as she flew past me.

Snow had started to fall again, drifting lazily from the sky. I walked up the steps, turning at the sound of a car coming down the driveway. When I recognized Dallas'

SUV, my heart clenched and my belly coiled with tension. Fuck. My plan had been to be gone before he showed up. Thea had said he wouldn't be here until tomorrow. Well, whatever. I didn't have to let him inside. Molly had raced to the door with me, so I let her in.

"Be right there, Molly."

I turned and waited, watching as Dallas rounded the circle in front of the house and came to a stop. My heart was beating so hard, it hurt. I told myself I could get through this. Hell, I'd gotten through walking in on my ex-fiancé screwing one of my friends. I could manage this too.

Dallas climbed out of his car. I watched him approach, my heart squeezing tight and my pulse racing. I knew I could get through this, but I didn't want to. It had been much easier to ignore my feelings for him when I didn't have to see him. He stopped at the foot of the stairs, looking up at me. He looked tired. His dark hair was rumpled and he had a shadow of stubble. His blue gaze pierced my heart. Dammit. He was so handsome. Why did my body have to respond so powerfully to him? Just having him near, and I wanted him like mad.

"Hi," he said simply.

I couldn't seem to speak, so I nodded,

swallowing against the knot of emotion in my throat. After a breath, I managed to form words. "Hi, what are you doing here?" I asked.

"I came to see you."

I shook my head quickly. "I don't think that's a good idea."

I heard Molly whining behind the front door and saw Dallas' eyes flick to the door and back to me. I knew she could hear his voice, and of course she wanted to see him. A childish, petty part of me didn't want to allow that. In part, because seeing him with her only reminded me his love of dogs was yet another reason I loved him. I wasn't that immature though, so I turned and opened the door. Molly dashed out, dancing in circles around him. He grinned and knelt down to greet her while she bathed his face in kisses. After she was satisfied, she dashed off into the yard again, galloping through the snow. He straightened, his eyes locking to mine again.

"Is it okay if I come in?" he asked.

"Dallas, I don't think that's a good idea. I'm not sure why you're here. Thea's not expecting you until tomorrow."

"I'm not here to see Thea today. I'm here to see you," he said simply.

Just the sound of his voice, low and gruff, sent shivers through me. Fuck. I was so screwed. Before I thought about what I was doing, I was opening the door and gesturing for him to follow me. At the last second, Molly came dashing up the stairs and through the door. As usual, she raced to the kitchen, and I could hear her lapping at her water bowl. Inside of a few more seconds, she dashed upstairs. Her favorite place to sleep was still at the foot of my bed. I supposed she felt safe there.

I toed off my boots and hung my jacket. Dallas stood right where he was in the entryway, waiting. I sighed. I'd let him in the door, so I might as well let him actually come in for a few minutes.

"Come on in. I'll be right back."

I heard him taking off his shoes and hanging his jacket as I walked through the dining room into the kitchen and then the bathroom. Closing the door, I took a deep breath and quickly washed my hands. Glancing at myself in the mirror, I sighed. I was a mess. My hair was falling out of its ponytail, I had dust streaked on my cheek, and I looked tired. I hadn't been sleeping well, not since Dallas had left. I splashed some water on my face, quickly dried it with a towel and returned to the kitchen.

Dallas was standing with his hips resting against the counter and his hands curled over the edge of it. His eyes met mine. I'd never seen him look uncertain, but that was how he looked at the moment. I gestured to the kitchen table. "Have a seat."

He pushed away from the counter and sat down facing me where I stood in the center of the kitchen.

"I'll make some coffee," I said, restless at the feel of his gaze on me.

Once the coffee was brewing, I sat down and looked over at him.

"What do you want Dallas?" I asked directly, ignoring the wild pounding of my heart and the joy that wanted to bubble up at seeing him.

"I wanted a chance to talk to you."

"Well, we're here. Talk. I'm not sure what else there is to say."

His shoulders rose and fell with a deep breath. He leaned back in his chair. "Look, I don't know how to do this," he finally said.

"How to do what?"

I truly didn't know what he meant to say.

"When you said you loved me," he paused, swallowing audibly before continuing. "I didn't know what to say. Not because I don't feel the same way..."

My heart lunged and nearly jumped up and down, banging against my ribs almost painfully. Hope soared wildly inside, like birds taking flight into the sky. I cut in. "What do you mean you feel the same way?"

He stared back at me for a long moment before he spoke, the moment so tense I thought I might explode. "I mean I love you too. But my life is the way it is. I suppose I can change it, but I don't know if I can be the man you deserve," he finally said.

It was clear the words didn't come easy for him. I stared at him, trying to collect my thoughts. The cacophony in my heart was hard to think above, but I was trying to focus on what he said because it mattered. A lot. It was the boundary he'd put up, and it was silly and pointless. "Dallas, you don't have to change anything to be the man I deserve," I finally said, my words coming out raspy with the emotion thundering inside of me.

He shook his head. "No you need someone whose job isn't so crazy they're rolling out of bed in the middle of the night. You need someone..."

I cut him off with a sharp shake of my head. "Stop it, Dallas. I know who you are. I know what your job is. It's part of what I admire and love about you. I don't need somebody around 24/7. I love you the way you are. I know your job is a part of your life. I can deal with it. It's not like my job isn't busy too. I work late and have cases that tie up extra time too. Look, I almost married Matthew and all he did was legal stuff for rich jerks. He had long hours and his work wasn't nearly as important as yours. It's not quantity, it's quality."

I didn't quite know how I sounded so certain, but I was. In this moment, I realized Dallas was as vulnerable as I was and somehow that made me feel stronger. It also made my heart ache for him. He'd walled himself off from everyone who mattered.

He stared at me, his eyes considering, and then he leaned forward, reaching for my hand. After a beat, he swore and stood, pulling me up from my chair and into his arms.

"It's been the longest damn week of my life," he murmured into my hair.

I sighed, tension unspooling inside. Finally held tight against him, his warmth and strength surrounding me, I could let go. Tears welled up, one sliding down my cheek.

I rubbed my cheek against his shirt and leaned back to look up at him.

"This week sucked," I said bluntly.

His eyes met mine, dark and open. "I know. Trust me, I know. I'm sorry I was an idiot."

In a flash, his mouth was on mine. We tumbled into a place I only went with him—where desire and emotion collided. His tongue swept deeply into my mouth while his hands mapped my body. Within seconds, he was tugging at my clothes. We were frantic. He groaned when he flicked the clasp between my breasts, the calloused surface of his palms sending pleasure streaking through me as he cupped my breasts and laved my nipples with his tongue.

He suddenly lifted his head. "I need a bed," he said roughly.

Then, he was lifting me up against him. I curled my legs around his hips. I'd managed to get his shirt off, so I sighed at the feel of his hard strong body against mine.

He cleared the top step, his eyes catching mine. "I'm assuming Molly's in your bedroom."

At my nod, he shouldered through the door to the guest bedroom, kicking it shut behind him. Everything was a blur. We yanked at each other's clothes, leaving what was left strewn across the floor and falling onto the bed in a tangle. He was hard and hot, and it felt so good to have him against me. He rolled atop me, and I curled my legs around him, wanting him inside of me right away. His cock slid against my slick folds as he propped himself up on his elbows and brushed my hair out of my face.

"I missed you so fucking much," he said, his voice gruff.

Emotion was riding so high inside of me, I could hardly contain it. I nodded wordlessly. He dropped kisses on my neck, charting his way down my body with his lips. A scrape of his teeth on my nipple, a drag of his tongue on my belly, need coiling tightly in my center, bundling to a knot at the apex of my thighs and swirling through me. He pushed my thighs apart, dropping kisses on the sensitive skin inside. I was wild with need, my hips rocking, murmuring his name over and over. I cried out when he dragged a finger through my folds and sank it knuckle deep inside.

I was already so close to the edge, and then his mouth was on me, his fingers and tongue driving me wild. I came more quickly than I wanted, my release crashing over me hard and fast. He made his way back up my body, and his hips settled into the cradle of mine.

"Audrey," he murmured.

I dragged my eyes open, colliding with his navy gaze.

Chapter Thirty-One

DALLAS

Audrey's gaze met mine, a swirl of green, gold and nutmeg. I could feel her core calling to me, the slick heat of it kissing the head of my cock. I needed to see her when I sank inside this time. I adjusted the angle of my hips and sank into her creamy clench in one swift surge.

"I'm not sure I know how to do this," I said as I settled into her, finally feeling as if I was back where I belonged. This close to her, I lost track of where I ended and she began. Intimacy curled around us, wrapping us in its embrace.

"To do what?" she whispered, her voice husky with passion.

"To love you the way you should be loved," I murmured.

She lifted a finger and traced my brows, her touch light as a feather. Her hand slid down to cup my cheek, and she traced my lips with her thumb. All the while my heart thudded inside of my chest as I struggled to contain the heady mix of emotion and lust only she elicited in me.

"You're already doing it. Stop worrying."

It was a leap of faith to come here, a leap of faith to do any of this. But I'd already stepped off the edge, and there was no turning back.

"If you say so," I finally managed, dipping my head and bringing my lips to hers.

I drew my hips back, sinking into her again, savoring the throb of her channel around me. We tumbled into nothing but sensation as I stroked into her again and again. I felt her begin to tighten, the need building in her again. Her hips rose to meet mine with every stroke. I kept my eyes open and locked with hers the whole time, watching as they widened and she clamped down around my cock, crying my name out. I let go, my release thundering through me and pouring into her.

I collapsed against her, spent and utterly

exhausted, physically and emotionally. After a few minutes, I lifted my head, brushing her tangled hair away from her face.

One look in her eyes, and I remembered just how much of a hold she had on me. She owned me—body, heart and soul.

AUDREY

I walked up the stairs to Dallas' family home, kicking the snow off my boots when I reached the door. Fresh snow had fallen during the night, dusting the landscape with fairy dust. I stepped through the door, nudging it with my shoulder. I had a large basket filled with rolls and pies. Thea, being the whirlwind she was, had assigned various tasks for cooking today's Christmas dinner. We'd done most of the cooking and baking at my parents' home because the kitchen here was empty from when they'd moved out.

After Dallas had shown up two days before Christmas, I had changed my plans when he asked me to stay. Instead of visiting my parents, they were coming up here. Thea and I had stayed up late last night cooking in our kitchen. She'd carted the ham and a few casseroles here this morning to stay warm in the ovens, while I'd finished up the baking. The house had lost some of its empty feeling. The sheets had been pulled off the furniture. Dallas had left my parents' house this morning to meet Noah and Ian here to shovel off the stairs and make sure the heat was working.

My mind spun back to another conversation with him last night. He'd made a passing comment that he wasn't so sure we should do Christmas at their family's home. I'd recalled Thea's concern, which I shared, about how heavily their father's actions had weighed on him.

"Dallas, it's the best place for Christmas," I'd said.

He'd started to roll his eyes, but I'd caught his hand in mine across the table. "Instead of letting him ruin everything you had, take it back. Thea wants to do this, so let her and enjoy it."

He'd looked doubtful, but the tension had eased from his features. I was hoping today might show him it would feel better for them to enjoy Christmas here again.

I followed the sound of voices. Once I

stepped into the kitchen, my mother spun around from where she was standing by the island in the center of the room. This was a lovely old kitchen with tall ceilings, windows that let light splash in from the outside, and cabinets lining the walls with a massive island in the middle.

"Audrey!" my mother exclaimed as she hurried over, unloading the basket from my arms. I had made cheese rolls, along with a pumpkin pie and an apple cherry pie. My mother, Sarah, pulled me tight for a hug.

"Hey Mom, I'm so glad you and Dad could drive up today."

Her silvery hair was wound into an elegant knot atop her head with loose tendrils hanging around her face. Her brown eyes crinkled at the corners with her smile. She tended to dress in rich colors, and today was no exception. She had on black slacks with a wine red sweater. When she stepped back, she angled her head to the side.

"So, Dallas?" she asked.

I felt my cheeks heat. "Not now, Mom. Okay?"

She laughed softly and leaned over to drop another kiss on my cheek. "It's okay. I think it's perfect. He called your father last night."

Dallas had told me he wanted to call my father because he didn't want to hide anything. I had felt a bit strange about it, but he insisted he wouldn't feel right not having everything out in the open. My father came meandering over and pulled me into a quick hug.

"Hi, dear," he said gruffly. "Very good to see you. Before you ask, the drive was uneventful. The snow stopped early this morning in Massachusetts."

My mother nudged him as Dallas walked into the kitchen from the back door. Dallas' cheeks were ruddy from the cold. One look at him sent my pulse lunging and heat rolling through me. My body had no regard for where we were.

My heart squeezed in my chest. It was hard to believe yesterday I'd woken up still wrestling with how much I missed him and yet determined to accept it and move on. In the span of twenty-four hours, joy and a sense of peace had fallen over me. His eyes caught mine from across the room as he shrugged out of his jacket. Noah and Ian were right behind him. All of the Tate siblings shared almost black hair. Thea and Dallas shared bright blue eyes, while Noah had dark brown eyes, and Ian had piercing green eyes.

I tried to recall the last time I'd seen them all together. It had been years since the last holiday season before their father went to jail. I recalled Dallas had seemed out of sorts then. I realized now, he'd probably been deep into the financial investigation and might've already known of his father's involvement. It was heartwarming to see them all together once again.

Noah glanced my way, flashing a grin, his eyes crinkling at the corners. "Hey Audrey. Long time no see."

I stepped to his side, and he pulled me into a quick hug with Ian right behind him. It was strangely familiar to be here. Our families had spent many holiday gatherings together. The early afternoon passed quickly as we bustled around the kitchen. By some miracle, Noah had finagled a television and the guys were watching football. We were all scattered around the living room. We'd eschewed a formal meal at the dining room table.

I was in the middle of a conversation with Thea and my mother when Dallas slipped onto the love seat beside me, his arm sliding across my shoulders. A sense of comfort rolled through me, and I glanced up. His bright blue gaze locked with mine. Sweet hell. It was ridiculous the effect he had on me. It didn't matter that his family and mine surrounded us. I would be perfectly content to find somewhere to sneak away.

My mother laughed, and we both looked in her direction. She smiled softly.

"It's nice to see you two together. A while back, I wondered," she commented.

"Wondered what?" Thea asked.

My mother lifted her shoulder and a shrug. "Oh, I saw the way they used to look at each other. I figured perhaps for Audrey it was nothing more than a crush, but I didn't know. I always thought you two would make a good match," she said with a satisfied smile before taking a sip of wine.

The afternoon rolled into evening with plenty of food and wine. At some point as darkness swept in and the stars glittered over the ocean, I was in the kitchen washing up. I felt Dallas come up behind me, his arms sliding down my shoulders to curl around my waist. I was elbow deep in soapy water and glanced up to the side.

"Yes?" I asked.

He dropped a kiss on the side of my neck, sending a hot shiver through me. Goose bumps prickled over my skin.

I glanced at him sideways, needing to ask

something. "So are you glad Thea rounded you all up for Christmas here?"

His eyes held mine, a grin curling the corner of his mouth. "Yes. You were right. Happy?"

I laughed, my heart feeling full. "Yes, but not because I was right. Just because it's a good thing for you."

He chuckled, dipping his head again and dropping more kisses along the sensitive skin of my neck.

"I think we should sneak away," he murmured.

"You've got to be kidding me," I said with a laugh.

Not to be deterred, he spun me around. I splashed water and soap on his shirt.

He shook his head, his eyes dark. "Not kidding at all. This house is huge. Come on," he murmured, dipping his head and dropping hot kisses along my collarbone. I couldn't have said no if my life depended on it.

"Hang on," I choked out. "Let me dry my hands."

Between giggles and a few gasps, I quickly grabbed the dishtowel and dried my hands. I let him tug me upstairs. I knew this house well because I'd spent so much time here when I was younger. One room I'd only seen and never been in was his old bedroom. Next thing I knew, he was pulling me through that door, his eyes hot on me. He'd spent every step of the way here being naughty with his hands. I was flustered and hot and wet. We yanked at each other's clothes after he kicked the door shut behind us. I moaned at the feel of his hot skin, his cock hard as steel in my palm. We tumbled onto the bed. The mattress was bare, but it was a bed.

He rolled atop me, lacing his fingers into mine and stretching my arms up over my head. The feel of his cock sliding against my wet folds sent a shudder through me.

"Dallas, don't make me..."

"Wait," he finished for me the second he filled me.

I cried out, the delicious stretch of his cock so good, I almost came instantly.

He didn't make me wait, the sweet crash of my release coming swiftly as he pounded into me.

"Merry Christmas," he murmured a few minutes later when he collapsed against me.

EPILOGUE

Dallas

I slid the key into the lock of our townhouse in Boston, opening the door quietly. It was much later than I wanted to be home. My work habits had changed drastically in the last year. In a week, Audrey and I would be driving up to Haven's Bay to spend our first Christmas together since we'd gotten married. In the year since last Christmas, Audrey had spent a few months in New York City before finally moving to Boston. I'd hated every day we'd been apart, but we'd spent weekends together. She'd accepted a position here in Boston working for the Environmental Protection Agency. She'd insisted on waiting until she had a position she wanted before she moved. I'd offered to relocate, but she preferred Boston because we could easily drive to Maine on weekends.

It was only eight o'clock, but for me, this was late. Since she'd moved here, I tried to be home by six every evening.

"Audrey," I called.

"In here," she called back.

Just the sound of her voice made me happy. I toed off my shoes, shrugged off my jacket and walked into the kitchen. It smelled divine. I had no idea what she was making, but she'd spoiled me rotten with her cooking ever since she moved in. We'd married last summer in a simple ceremony. She hadn't wanted to plan an elaborate wedding, telling me she'd already had enough of that with her first engagement. Audrey's parents, Thea, Noah and Ian had been our witnesses and then we had a dinner party the following day up in Haven's Bay.

Audrey spun to face me. Her hair was up in a messy knot, tendrils framing her face, and her skin was flushed. She had flour all over her shirt. No matter how much she loved cooking, she never wore an apron, which I found endlessly amusing. I stepped to her side and tugged her close.

She giggled. "I'm getting flour all over you."

"I don't care. Missed you today," I murmured, dipping my head to kiss the side of her neck. I closed my eyes and breathed in the scent of her—honey with a hint of vanilla. I sighed at the feel of her soft body coming against mine. One small thing kept her a little further away. She was six months pregnant, and it showed.

"How are you feeling?" I asked sliding my hand over the curve of her belly.

"I feel fine every day. You worry too much," she said with a low laugh.

She'd declared the other day she was putting a restriction on how often I could ask how she was feeling. I couldn't help it. I couldn't have known I'd love her being pregnant so much. We didn't know whether it was a boy or girl and had agreed we'd wait to find out. We wanted the surprise. My heart clenched every time I looked at her. My life felt so full, I didn't quite know what to do with it sometimes. I absolutely adored her pregnant. With her full breasts and her round belly—I had no shame, I got hard just thinking about her. For example, right now. She glanced up when my hard cock bumped against her hip.

"You are too much. I'm finishing cooking before we do anything else," she announced with a roll of her eyes as she pushed against me.

But I saw the heat flashing there.

"I don't think so," I said, pulling her back and dropping kisses down along her neck. In short order, I dragged her down the hall into our bedroom. I was spooned behind her, buried deep inside her. I felt her shuddering, her channel clenching around me as my release poured into her. We laid there, my hand resting over the curve of her belly, cupping one of her breasts. I thought I could die happy right there. Except I wanted more—of her and everything that came with her.

———

Thank you for reading All I Want - I hope you loved Dallas & Audrey's story!

For more holiday romance, check out Truly Madly Mine, my upcoming release in the Swoon Series. Dani and Wade have what some might call *history*. It all ended with a slushy thrown in high school.

As fate would have it, they end up working together years later. Despite Dani's best intentions, she just *might* still have a thing for Wade.

Wade just *might* do anything to get her back. When he finally gets his chance, he grabs it with both hands. Buckle up for a smoking hot second chance, friends to lovers, holiday romance!

Keep reading for a sneak peek!

Be sure to sign up for my newsletter for the latest news, teasers & more! Click here to sign up: http://jhcroixauthor.com/subscribe/

Dani

My hand slipped just as I brought down a bag of flour from the shelf above me. The heavy bag bounced off another shelf and exploded, sending a cloud of flour all over me.

I opened my mouth—to provide a choice curse—only to inhale a breath of flour. A coughing and sneezing fit ensued. When I finally caught me breath, I leaned against the wall with a sigh, not even bothering to deal with the torn bag of flour on the floor.

"Bless you," a voice said from the doorway.

Fuck my life.

Opening my eyes, I glanced down to see my apron and my hands and arms dusted white. Lifting a hand, I patted my hair, sending a burst of flour into the air again. I only hoped the flour I felt on my face obscured my blush when I lifted my eyes to meet the teasing gaze of Wade Ellis.

"Thanks," I said, instantly wishing my tone didn't come out so sharp. "Remind me who's idea it was to store the flour above my head."

Wade's grin stretched wider, and my pulse —rather disobedient by the way—took off at a fast gallop. Meanwhile, a funny spinning feeling happened in my belly. There were many things I could control. The state of my body when Wade teased me was not one of them, despite my best efforts.

"Now that, I don't know. The kitchen is definitely your zone. I'm sure it was your idea."

A little laugh broke loose. Because I couldn't help it. Even if I hated that Wade happened to find me in this state, I knew he was right. I *was* bossy and didn't mind owning it. I was certain I'd had a good reason for storing the flour there, but it seemed foolish now.

"What are you doing here so early this morning anyway?" I asked, glancing around for a towel.

My eyes landed on a stack of clean dish

towels just by the door, and I pushed away from the wall to reach for one.

"I'm leading a long hike today," Wade replied. "Came by to stock up on some first aid supplies."

When I lifted my hand to brush the towel over my flour-covered hair, my bracelet caught on the elastic holding my ponytail in place. "Dammit," I murmured as I moved too quickly, almost yanking the elastic out.

Wade's low chuckle send heat chasing over my skin like little licks of fire. "Hang on, let me help," he said, stepping closer.

My pulse went absolutely wild, my breath hitched in my throat and a flush of heat blasted me from head to toe. I spent a lot of time not getting too close to Wade.

All that effort was wasted. He stood right at my side, his presence intense. He exhibited an easy strength and grace no matter what he did. When I moved to try to untangle my bracelet, my elbow bumped into his muscled chest, and I almost exclaimed. Dear God, his chest was truly nothing but muscle.

My mouth did what it always did when I was around Wade and started babbling. "Geez, dude. Working out enough?" I asked, my tone sarcastic.

I felt his hands carefully untangling a few

curls in the elastic around my bracelet. "You know my job keeps me in shape," he murmured in reply. The contrast of his hard body and having this massive bear of a man carefully untangling my hair made my heart squeeze a little. "There, it's going to be easiest if I just pull it out."

I lowered my arms and waited, my curls falling in a wild tangle around my shoulders as he extricated the hair band. Wade stepped back, holding up the elastic. When I took it from him, my fingers brushed against his, sending a hot jolt of electricity up my arm.

We stood there staring at each other. The normally busy staff kitchen at the lodge restaurant was quiet as dawn hadn't even arrived. It wasn't even 5:30 a.m. yet. It felt as if Wade and I were all alone in the world, caught in this little bubble. The air felt as if it were firing sparks around us.

The usual teasing look in Wade's eyes faded as he searched my face. His espresso gaze darkened. A stillness fell over me as I looked at him, letting my eyes travel over the strong, clean lines of his face. Wade was all man and tall with broad shoulders. His dark brows angled up slightly. His cheekbones were a thing of beauty—bold, sculpted curves. His perfectly straight nose was centered over his full lips. His square jaw had a shadow of stubble on it.

My fingers tingled with the urge to lift my hand and cup his cheek. I didn't know what the hell was going on with me. I couldn't seem to move. I was frozen, my breath coming in shallow little pants as I stared up at Wade. The space in the pantry was quiet for several long beats, all the while I could hear the rush of blood in my ears with every beat of my heart.

"Dani."

I heard my name on Wade's lips but it had been years since I'd heard that tone in his voice. It was rough, laced with need.

I felt caught in a current that spun into itself. The need to finally give into what I'd been denying myself for years was so overpowering, I couldn't seem to call upon my snarky self and push back against it.

In a hot second, my head tipped back just as Wade leaned down. His lips brushed across mine when he murmured my name again, the whisper of his voice sending an electric tingle over my lips that raced through every cell in my body. I felt it course through me, sparking from the inside out.

A frayed sigh escaped. Then, Wade fit his

mouth over mine. One fiery second burned into another, everything going up in flames.

This wasn't the first time I had kissed Wade. Not even close. Our young, messy kisses in high school didn't hold a candle to this one. It was quite clear Wade had some practice in the intervening years. He kissed me like he was born to it—sensual strokes of his tongue against mine, his hand lacing into my hair as he angled my head to the side and devoured my mouth.

I wasn't passive, oh no. I wanted this too much. Denial might've work for a while— hell, even for years—but once the gates fell, all hell broke loose.

I was lost in the kiss, the feeling of his strong, hard body holding mine against his, and the taste of him was intoxicating. Sweet Jesus, his kisses had set me on fire inside and out.

"Hey Dani, do you—" The question stopped abruptly. "Oh! Oh my!"

The sound of footsteps hurrying away from the pantry echoed as Wade and I broke apart, our breath coming in sharp heaves.

We stared at each other. Oh my God.

———

Available now!
Truly Madly Mine

If you love steamy, small town romance, take a visit to Willow Brook, Alaska in my Into The Fire Series. Check out Burn For Me - a second chance romance for the ages. It's FREE on all retailers! Don't miss Cade & Amelia's story!

Go here to sign up for information on new releases: http://jhcroixauthor.com/subscribe/

5) Follow me on Instagram at https://www.instagram.com/jhcroix/

6) Like my Facebook page at https://www.facebook.com/jhcroix

———

Swoon Series
This Crazy Love
Wait For Me
Break My Fall
Truly Madly Mine
Still Go Crazy - coming February, 2020!
Into The Fire Series
Burn For Me
Slow Burn
Burn So Bad
Hot Mess
Burn So Good
Sweet Fire
Play With Fire
Melt With You
Burn For You
Crash & Burn
Brit Boys Sports Romance
The Play
Big Win
Out Of Bounds
Play Me

Naughty Wish
Diamond Creek Alaska Novels
When Love Comes
Follow Love
Love Unbroken
Love Untamed
Tumble Into Love
Christmas Nights
Last Frontier Lodge Novels
Take Me Home
Love at Last
Just This Once
Falling Fast
Stay With Me
When We Fall
Hold Me Close
Crazy For You
Just Us
Catamount Lion Shifters
Protected Mate
Chosen Mate
Fated Mate
Destined Mate
A Catamount Christmas
The Lion Within
Lion Lost & Found

ACKNOWLEDGMENTS

This story started with nothing more than the idea of a snowy night and two hearts colliding. It turned into a little more than that when Dallas strolled into my thoughts. I had a poll with you, my most fabulous readers, and you voted for Dallas to get his holiday happily-ever-after.

Hugs & kisses to every single one of you who cheers on my books! I love hearing from you, so never hesitate to give me a shout. As always, my proofreader angels - Janine, Beth P., Terri D., Terri E., & Heather H. make sure I don't look too silly once a book is out in the wild. Laura Kingsley edits with a keen eye and doesn't allow me to let my characters down. Meanwhile, Yoly Cortez makes my books shine with her artful eye and stunning cover design.

To my dogs who contribute to every book I write with lots of love, wags, and paws on my keyboard. They also make sure I get out for a run - rain, wind, sleet, snow, or sun - every single day, which is usually when I plot my stories. That's when Molly, the sweet stray, came into this story.

Last, but certainly not least, my ever-patient husband. He graciously shares opinions on everything from cover models to cover fonts and reliably helps me name things when I'm stuck. All my love.

xoxo

J.H. Croix